# LONG DELAYED JUSTICE

## ALEC PECHE

# ACKNOWLEDGMENTS

I'd like to thank Alanna Weaver and Vera Chan for brainstorming ideas for this book.

I'd like to thank my editors GM and Ellen Falk. Both of you must wonder when I'll learn to use 'that' versus 'who' in a sentence. I'm afraid the answer is likely never. It's the way my brain is wired. Sigh.

# CHAPTER 1

"*I* need your help with a cold case," retired Detective Natalie Severino said over the phone line.

Damian Green had been happily lost in tinkering with a new invention of his when she called. "Yes?"

"I heard that sigh in your voice, Damian. You know the PD would love to hire you full time to help them solve crimes."

"Natalie, you're wasting my time if you called to harass me with that question. The answer to the PD's question is a forever 'no.' I did you all a favor by hiring Jordan to develop the software for all PDs. That's my contribution. What cold case do you need help with? Specifically, what do you need me for?"

Natalie Severino retired from the San Jose Police Department over five years ago and now worked part-time in the cold case unit. When Natalie was a detective, she solved the murder of Damian's wife and two children and eventually shot the suspect dead. He appreciated that she'd spared him a court case.

"This case actually is fifteen years old. Because it's a murder case, there is no statute of limitation on it. We have a man on video who was caught murdering a shopkeeper. Over the years, officers have worked the case and come up with no leads. The man did not leave DNA behind and at the time we didn't have facial recognition software. We do now, but we get so many hits on it that we can't do anything with the information. I was thinking your software might be better, or you might be able to tell the computer to do something different than the police computers do."

Damian smiled at the vision that Natalie was painting. He chuckled to himself with the thought of walking down to his lower level and talking to his computer. It was something like talking to Hal in the movie *2001: A Space Odyssey*. Unlike the movie, his computer would do nothing. He had not set it up to take voice commands. His computer would be confused with his out-loud musings. It was far better to develop a program in a language the computer understood. Natalie was correct, though, that his computer would be better at the search than the police computer. He thought he could search for the guy based on his original picture with a little pixel touch-up and by letting the computer age him to take a guess at what he looked like now.

"I can help. Send me over any video coverage you have of your suspect. I have a few different ways I can handle the picture. I also have technology that will age him, but do you have a police sketch of what he looks like now? Also, were there any street videos at the time or any information about how he departed? If he stole cash, what is the record on that cash? Do you have a video for the week prior in case he came in and cased the joint? I believe that's how cops talk."

"Yes, the crime scene unit collected the video for the prior week. There's no record on the cash as this was a corner store with people walking in and out all the time paying with cash. I'll send you that information and what the detectives have collected over the years."

"Okay. I'll read what you have and drop you a note on how my search for your suspect went. I'll also let you know if I have any other ideas outside of this facial search. I would think if he murdered during a small store robbery that he is a career criminal, so I'll also check a few prison databases."

"I'd ask how you do that, but I don't think I want to know."

Damian chuckled and they ended their call.

Damian looked at the time and noted it was getting toward late afternoon in September. Hermione had track practice and then driver education training, so he would not see his ward or Ariana Knowles, his girlfriend and his ward's other temporary parent, that evening. He was free to work on the case for Natalie. He had to think that the department was giving her the most difficult detective cold cases to solve knowing that she would bring him in on the case. They had made him a serious employment offer to which he politely said no. Really, though, they were getting a good deal—they got his computer skills for free, and better still, since he wanted to stay out of the spotlight, their department looked really smart at closing cold cases.

He had another hour of work at his warehouse in Richmond, California, before he headed to the harbor to return to his island home—Red Rock Island. It was located close to the Richmond San Rafael Bridge in San Francisco Bay. It had been a difficult piece of land to build on, but he had quite a fortress and kept anyone off the island that he didn't want there. It was the perfect loner property. That was, until Ariana washed up on his shore when her scuba tank went dry. That was followed by the discovery of Hermione in the boat that he used to move between his island and the mainland. Her original name was Hannah, but they changed it to hide her identity and her choice was the character's name from a popular book. It had taken a couple of years to locate her parents who were in protective custody. His ward had made the decision to stay with him and Ariana rather than her parents. She was a teenager and had a far better life living in Belvedere with Ariana and occasionally on Red Rock Island with Damian. Recently he and Ariana began pursuing a romantic relationship.

He approached his island and used the remote to open his

watercraft garage. A deck folded out. He then got out onto the dock and attached a tow rope to the front of the boat to pull it into his makeshift garage for the night. Then he hit the button to retract the dock into its opening and the island was closed up for the night.

He walked through his lower level knowing he would work there later. He headed upstairs to check his refrigerator for food. He decided to fish for himself as well as his two cats, Bailey and Bella. A short time later, he had caught enough food for the three of them to enjoy a fish dinner. They followed him inside knowing he would filet and chop the raw fish for them first before cooking his own dinner. Later he took a beer downstairs with him to look at the information Natalie had promised to send.

He read the case notes, which really had a whole lot of nothing. Then he watched the video of the shopkeeper's death. It was hard to watch. It brought back thoughts of his family being murdered by a falsely released Soledad Prison convict. His wife and two daughters were murdered by gunshots. It had been nine years ago and he still felt the pain in his heart of his family not being on the island with him to enjoy the life he now had. He decided to edit the murder out of the video and see if he could still help solve the cold case for the police. He just couldn't keep watching the shopkeeper's death as he tried to find a photo with the best pixels and facial views. He used one type of software to enhance a series of pictures of the suspect from slightly different angles as he walked into the store.

Then he pulled up the video of the previous week to see if the man had indeed visited the store before he later came back and robbed it. When the suspect arrived for the robbery, he had a baseball cap low over his face, and kept his face turned down away from where he knew the camera was located. If he had visited the store before the robbery, he likely would have kept his head up searching for any cameras that would later catch the robbery. He programmed his facial recognition software to match the photo and to look for someone whose eyes were traveling around looking for cameras. He then pulled up his email while the computer went to work. He'd give Ariana and Hermione a call later to check in on them.

He barely got through his email before his computer program notified him it was done with the search. That was no surprise as the video wasn't that long and his computer was very powerful. He pulled up the results, smiled, and then forwarded the information to Natalie. He gave her five minutes, then picked up the phone.

"Hey, I was just sorting through the information you sent me. Your computer identified the suspect in ten minutes? That's unbelievable. Walk me through what you did. If this works out, the department will have to forward me another cold case because you're solving them so quickly."

"I'll have to start limiting you to one case every two weeks. I do feel good when the cases are solved, but this suspect is already behind bars serving a life sentence, so no satisfaction there."

"Well, there will be satisfaction for the family and the department. So how did your computer find this guy?"

"Satisfaction won't bring back their father, but I hear you, Natalie. I have a program that adds pixels to photographs by doing a probability on features. I then asked the computer to match the walk and look for someone who was searching for ceiling cameras. It did that, and when he first cased the joint, his features were caught very well on camera. I have no idea if this is enough to convict someone, but it wouldn't hurt to send a few detectives to Pelican Bay and see if they can coerce the prisoner into a confession," Damian said.

"I'll let the LT know and they can take it from there. They would let me go with them, but I hate that prison. It's a SuperMax State Prison with the worst of the worst, kept in nearly inhumane conditions."

"Wait, Natalie, are you sympathetic to prisoners?"

"No. It's just depressing to see such a waste of a lifetime. I'd want to commit suicide if that was my life day in, day out. I don't know what else we can do with such horrible human beings, but Pelican Bay would not be my answer. Besides, it is in the middle of nowhere just south of the Oregon border. Someone else can interview the guy."

"Okay, well good luck and goodnight."

"Goodnight."

Damian sat back and stretched his six-foot frame, shoving his white-blond hair away from his eyes. He'd have to schedule a haircut soon. He wondered if Natalie would call him back with a new cold case the next day. Her Lieutenant would be pleased the case was solved so quickly, and he'd want Natalie to take a crack at a new case. Damian wondered if his work represented enough evidence to consider the case closed. He also wondered if they would bother with a trial as the guy was already serving a life sentence. What would be the point? Maybe they could get the guy to sign a statement confessing to the murder so at least the family of the victim would consider it closed. Oh well, it wasn't his problem.

He turned on the TV to watch a game between his favorite team—the Golden State Warriors and the San Antonio Spurs. It was a year when the Warriors appeared to be dominating the competition. He enjoyed the energy from Steph Curry and the zeal of Draymond Green. At halftime, he called Ariana to check on her and Hermione.

"Hey there, how's it going?"

"We're doing well. Hermione memorized the Driver's Education booklet and knows more rules of the road than I do."

"How's her sense of awareness and peripheral vision? You need that to avoid idiots on the road."

"She's, of course, excellent at both of those things. She'll get her provisional permit next month and I feel comfortable letting her drive as much as she wants."

"Have you taken her across the Golden Gate Bridge at rush hour or through the hilly streets of San Francisco? Belvedere is a quiet and low-traffic city."

"I haven't, but she always has nerves of steel, so I don't anticipate trouble. You can take her driving on the weekend. Will you be over this weekend?" Ariana asked.

"I'm planning on it. Will she be around, or does she have a track meet or sleep-over with her friends?"

"No competition on the weekend, and she has other plans, but I suspect if you tell her she's going to drive across the bridge and into the city, you'll become her priority."

"Okay, I'll do that. What do you want to do this weekend? The three of us could go to Monterey or Carmel and we could let Hermione drive part of the way."

"That sounds like a plan. Let me call her to the phone."

Damian could tell he was put on hold momentarily while Ariana was calling their ward to the phone. A moment later he heard Hermione's voice.

"Hey, Damian what's up?" He pictured the lanky teenager with her short black bob. Her original hair was red, but when they first became her fake parents, they had her change her hair color and length for her own safety. They were beyond the safety issue, but she was used to the black hair.

"Ariana and I were thinking of taking a weekend trip to Monterey or Carmel. We were planning on having you chauffeur us there. Do you have an interest in going or do you have other plans?"

"I do have other plans, but nothing that can't be rescheduled. I'd rather play at being your chauffeur. I have to get fifty hours of supervised instruction, so a trip to Monterey would cross off perhaps six hours."

Damian chuckled, "Ever the calculating teen. You could have said, 'I love your company and would gladly give up my friends to spend time with you two.'"

"I know you wouldn't fall for that line, otherwise I might have tried it."

"That's backward praise from a teenager, so I'll take it. What else is going on? Do you like your classes this week?" Damian asked.

"They're getting a bit harder. This semester I have three advanced placement classes so they're harder than last year."

"Are you going to get a 'B' in one of those classes?"

"Not if I can help it. I have a perfect record and I want to keep it that way," Hermione said.

"Yay, for you! What else is going on?"

"Not much. Track and field practice is somewhat boring. All we do is run."

"Ah, isn't that the point? Whether you are doing short distances or long, the only way to improve your technique is to practice. What are you thinking of competing in for the track team?"

"I'm not sure. The conditioning would help me with other sports, but if I want to be a better goalie, perhaps I should try the high jump, pole vaulting, or the long jump."

"Wow, those are different events than I was thinking of, but they are track skills. If you want to be a better soccer goalie, I would guess that the long jump is the best event to prepare you as you learn to jump in the air long distances. The body positions are wrong for high jump and pole vaulting. I don't know, Kiddo. What does the track coach say?"

"She says that the long jump would be good for me and that I don't have the right body type for the bar events. Apparently, I need to be short-waisted and long-legged for the high jump and tall for the pole vault. I'm average in both those areas. She also said that I might look at short-distance hurdles as I need to be fast and have to leap. So I'm just confused. Can you help?"

"Why don't I look at the background of famous soccer goalies and see what high school sports they did? As many goalies are from Europe, I don't know if they have comparable high school sports, but I'll ask the computer to run a mini-program so you can have the analytics to help make your decision. However, you should do what sport you enjoy, or maybe none if it is boring you."

"Thanks, Damian, I would like to know those analytics. I'll tell my coach what you're doing and see if she needs any other analytics."

"Sure. I'd be happy to help, but only if you're enjoying these sports."

"I enjoy competing. I guess I'm frustrated since I don't know where to focus. The track choices are many, and there are just a few things I don't want to try like the shot put, but I need to narrow my focus more."

"I'll also run a program on track schedules. Perhaps you can do more than one event, but that would only work if they don't get scheduled at the same time. So, there's another piece of information to help you focus."

"Cool. I don't know why I didn't think to ask you for that stuff before. Gotta run and do my homework. Here's Ariana."

"You do realize that you managed to engage her for more than thirty seconds, which is a rarity in her age group. Also, on my end of the phone, she wasn't scrolling through her phone while talking to you. Congratulations!"

"The conversation was destined to last your standard thirty seconds until I asked her about the track team. That appealed to her mind, and she extended the conversation an extra thirty seconds," Damian said with a chuckle.

"Ah, she's confused about that sport and because she's confused, it's taking away from her enjoyment. Sounds like you might have a way to clear her head on that one."

They continued their discussion finalizing plans for the weekend, looking at some rentals in each city and settled on Carmel, then ended the call.

# CHAPTER 2

It was mid-week before he heard from Natalie again.

"Hey Damian, how's it going?"

"Good at the moment. I read the story about the SJPD closing that cold case quickly. I assume the guy confessed."

"Yes, and everyone's happy and the family somewhat relieved. Mostly it's just sad at the waste of the life—the shopkeeper who died well before his time and the murdering convict serving out a life sentence."

"So, you called me because you have a new cold case? I thought your superiors were going to wait at least two weeks before assigning you a new case. Your part-time retirement job is turning into a full-time gig."

"Actually, they decided to try and stretch my relationship with you. They would like help on a current case. Let me give you the highlights and then, if you agree to help, I'll walk into a conference room that contains the investigative units of the DA, SJPD, and County leadership."

"Wow, Natalie, that's some pressure. Tell me a little about the case and I'll see if there's an avenue I can help with."

"So, I don't have to tell you this is a confidential conversation since you normally want your assistance to the SJPD to remain a secret, but the DA wanted me to say that. Okay, they have a problem with the locally elected sheriff. They have collected information around the edges that links her to many illegal things including harassment, extortion, embezzlement, and murder. As county sheriffs are elected, it takes a recall election to get them out of office. They can't just be fired by another government official."

"Wow, all that and the person is elected?"

"Not only elected as sheriff, but before this, she was a school board member, a city council member, the mayor, an SJPD officer, and a county supervisor. She has her tentacles into everything and a war chest of campaign funds to keep the status quo."

"Okay, how can I help?"

"We need more information from common sources you can reach, as well as, I believe the DA said, 'the dark web.' Those are his words, not mine."

"Yes, I've dabbled in the dark web. Don't they have infinite computer resources to do this research?"

"Normally, they do. However, as I said, the suspect has her tentacles everywhere and a few of the investigators looking into her past have disappeared. We have leaks in our departments, so this group wants you to help because you are extremely capable, and almost as importantly, you won't leak."

Damian could see the problem. He could swear he'd read about it happening a few other times. He liked to think of politicians as octopuses. They had their arms and hands stretched out for money and power all the time.

"Okay, I'll bite. Take me into your conference room. I'd rather do this on a video call as I'd like to watch the body language of those in the room. Can you arrange that?"

"It will take a few minutes, but I can arrange that. I'll text or email you a link."

"Okay."

After they ended their conversation, Damian thought about how much he hated crooked politicians. He'd be happy to assist in getting rid of one of them. He just wondered if everyone on this small task force was clean. Oh well, he would warn them he would be checking on them.

A few minutes later and he was dialing into a conference room and looking at some faces he recognized and others that were new to him.

"Hello."

"Mr. Green, thank you for joining us. I'm DA Jeffrey Silverstein. I'll make introductions," said a slim man who appeared to be in his late forties with hair greying at his temples and looking very lawyerly.

Damian decided to strike first, "Natalie gave me a brief outline of your problem. I hate crooked politicians and the first thing I'll be doing is investigating all of you to make sure you won't be the source of a leak to the sheriff. Once I move beyond that, I'll help. What do you want help with for this investigation?"

There was a painful silence before the police chief came back and said, "Mr. Green, I appreciate your candor here and welcome it. I also want to thank you for the assistance you provided in closing other cases for the department. I believe you have powerful computers that can do more than one thing at once, and perhaps you have the ability to access our computers. So set them to investigate everyone in the room and will you also begin research on this case? Our suspect is Wendy Knight. She was two chiefs before me. She was accidentally shot about fifteen years ago during a hunting trip. She's in a wheelchair as she's a paraplegic. She wields the wheelchair to get the sympathy vote and to stop people from saying negative things about her. She's charismatic and has attracted followers like a cult."

"My office had explored charging her in the past, but just as we got close, evidence or a key witness disappeared," the DA continued with the story.

"What's different about this time, Mr. Silverstein?" Damian asked.

"Frankly, you, Mr. Green. Chief Swanson has described some of the information gatherings you've done in the past and that's what we need here. Also, we understand your home is quite fortified with security, so we don't worry about you disappearing. Meaner, tougher parties than Wendy Knight have tried, but they haven't been able to bring harm to you, and that's important to me, and indeed all the people in the room."

"I'm fortunate in that I have had other police agencies in other counties come to my rescue. Does your sheriff have friends in other agencies that might try and harm me?" Damian asked, thinking not of his house, but of Ariana and Hermione.

"She does have friends in other agencies. One of the people who disappeared lived in Solano County and another in San Mateo County," replied the chief.

"Hmmm. I've had Alameda, Contra Costa, and San Francisco law enforcement come to my aid. Should my land be attacked, will you commit a helicopter and officers to render aid? My island is fortified and will withstand most weapons, but I'd like to have aid when I need it. Certainly, I need help hauling away any criminals."

"I will commit protection to you even though it is out of our jurisdiction," the chief said, looking at the DA. "I think we have obscure laws that allow us to step over that jurisdiction to protect a key witness of ours."

The DA nodded his agreement.

"Okay, if you'll give me your full names during introductions, I'll check you out. Chief, Mr. Silverstein, if you'll proceed to tell me what you would like researched, I'll work on that at the same time," Damian said.

He could see tight lips and some red faces with his request, but Damian didn't care. He wondered if he would find that anyone in the room was dirty. Damian recorded the names on his end, and they proceeded to the group's request of how Damian could help. Damian had his powerful computers in motion searching the room's occupants by the time the chief explained what he wanted Damian's help with finding.

"Mr. Green, here are some of the data points we'd like researched."

"Please, call me Damian," he said after he finished writing down the list. "When is the next meeting of this group?" Damian asked, wondering about any deadlines. Given the leaks that were occurring during this investigation, he rather thought that the sooner he found information, the better for everyone involved.

"We'll meet as soon as you have anything substantial. We could meet tomorrow at the same time if you think you'll have anything by then," the police chief replied.

"It is likely that I'll have something by this time tomorrow. Should we plan on chatting then?"

The call ended shortly after Damian's remark, and he went to check his security system. This was not a time to be sloppy. He also took a look at Ariana's house as she needed to be safe as well. He texted her with the news that he was turning on a component of her system that she had not activated and the reason for his caution. She acknowledged the text, and they promised to talk later.

Damian reviewed the data his computer was generating, and he said, "Bingo." He watched a while longer to see if anything suspicious came up for anyone else. He picked up the phone to call Natalie. He didn't have the private numbers of the police chief and the DA. He asked her to get them to jointly call him at their convenience.

Natalie messaged him that the phone call would take place at seven that night. He finished working on the data for Hermione and chatted with Ariana before he sat down for the call with the police chief and district attorney.

"Mr. Green, you have something for us?" asked the DA after

everyone arrived on the video chat. It seemed that even though he'd told this group to call him Damian, they drifted toward the formal address.

"Yes, one of your committee persons is likely the source of leaks to your sheriff. I was able to track payments made to an offshore account. It's either that or there's another politician in play, making payments in your local jurisdiction."

"Who is it?" asked Chief Theodore Swanson.

"Supervisor Santiago. He's got $250,000 in suspicious deposits. The deposits were made by the sheriff hidden under about five layers of accounts located in the Caymans."

"Can you show us your work to find that information? We'll need that to make any allegation of bribery or conspiracy. I looked into all the committee members before you joined us, and I found nothing."

"Did you look at offshore accounts?"

"Haven't a clue how to do that."

"Okay, well let me walk you through it."

By the time he was done, the DA said, "I can understand why you're such a help to the police. You dare to go to places we don't let our IT staff visit. We may need to re-think that policy as you haven't visited illegal locations; rather, you are examining risky internet locations, but gathering very good information."

"Yes, if you know where to look and have computing power behind you, you would be amazed what you can find through legal means."

"We'll serve a warrant on Mr. Santiago tonight, and he'll no longer attend our meetings on what to do with Sheriff Knight."

"See you in the morning," Damian said as he made to end the video call.

"Wait!" Damian heard the chief say just before he pushed his disconnect button.

"Yes, Chief?"

"Did your computers finish searching everyone?"

"Yes, why?" Damian asked.

"It just some days I feel like half of the people I deal with are corrupt. I guess I'm surprised you didn't find a second person with suspicious bank account deposits."

"I get where you're coming from, Chief; however, so far Mr. Santiago is the only problem member of that committee. I do have a search function set up for the other members of your committee in case they step over the line financially any time during this committee's work."

"Good to know. Thanks for the work you're doing, Mr. Green."

"Call me Damian, and you're welcome." This time Damian did hit the end call button.

Damian leaned back and thought about the case. Surely, given the presence of Mr. Santiago at the meeting, this sheriff was already marshaling her resources to come after him. He worried that the sheriff would also target his family, Ariana and Hermione. His name was on the school district listing as Hermione's father. When he and Ariana developed the scheme to get their ward registered for school, the only route they could think of was as parents rather than guardians, and thus they were registered that way with the school district. The sheriff would need to know that Damian had a ward and which school district she attended, as it wasn't the one that his island home was connected to. He thought he had a few more days of safety before Wendy Knight's minions caught up with him.

# CHAPTER 3

All was quiet on his island for nearly the remainder of the week. Damian completed compiling his data analysis of the athletes who competed in track and field and sent it to Hermione with a suggestion that she review it. Damian thought she might be best suited for the long jump event and the three-hundred-meter-high hurdles based on what he saw, but it was her choice. He bet it would come up in their discussion during their drive to Carmel that weekend.

He was fishing on Thursday evening to procure food for his two cats, Bailey and Bella, when he heard a sound and saw a drone heading his way. That was unusual. He decided to delay his fishing and head inside so he could determine where the drone came from. Normally he didn't see drones near his island as most operators didn't want to drop their drones into the water. If the drone ran out of battery power, it would drop into the bay and be destroyed.

He was on alert given the investigation he had joined with the San Jose police. His house was outside of their jurisdiction, but it sounded like this sheriff wasn't concerned with jurisdiction and would come after him at some point. He figured she was especially mad as he had her point person ejected from the committee, and that point person knew Damian's identity. In his basement lab, he pulled up the island's camera monitors to watch the drone's activity. His island was fortified with protective water sprays and drones that dropped things, and his house was made from bulletproof metal. He'd built it that way because although he was in the large metropolitan area of San Francisco Bay, it would take law enforcement precious minutes to assist him since he was offshore. He debated trying to shoot it down and decided to hold back on that idea. Then the drone came within five feet of his front door, and Damian lost his patience. He fired at it with one of many high-pressure hose outlets he had around his house and island for protection. This time he loaded his water pressure gun with castor oil and fired. The castor oil weighed down the drone copter blades and covered its camera lens, and then it dropped to the ground when the remote drone operator couldn't see to direct its motion. He quickly returned to the outside to capture the disabled drone. It was bouncing around on the dirt and he grabbed it and removed the battery and covered its lens with a black cloth. He returned to his lab to ensure that there wasn't a backup battery on the unit. He then returned outside to finish acquiring dinner for his cats.

Damian was an inventor of odd gadgets. In addition to his island's novel defense systems and building design, he had a prototype device that refrigerated his cats' food and dispensed it as frequently as required. He enjoyed the company of the cats and wanted them taken care of when he spent a night off the island. They likely could fish for themselves, but the water in the bay was cold and he knew they didn't like it. There were no mice or rats for them to catch as most of the island was formed from rock. He also didn't want them hungry enough to pick off the odd bird that visited the island. He finished collecting the fish for his cats, adding other ingredients for a homemade recipe, then returned downstairs to review the drone.

He looked up the drone model online and read about its features. He was happy to see that it had a built-in camera. He hoped it was launched by a dumb operator as that would mean they turned on the camera immediately which would give Damian their identity. After cleaning off the drone, he found a connector wire to download the camera footage. He hit the jackpot when viewed the video footage. He saw a group of people at the drone's launch with clear enough pictures that he would be able to use facial-recognition software to identify them. He followed the video over the harbor and to his island. The footage captured his back as he entered his house. He was pleased that it hadn't caught the source of the damage he inflicted on the drone. It was better if he didn't reveal the secrets of his island security system.

He returned to the beginning of the video and discovered footage from another sheriff's event on the video. It showed officers serving a piece of paper, but nothing more happened after the occupant took the piece of paper and closed the door. He put the pictures of the group through his identity software. One was a sheriff's deputy and, after a little more research, he discovered the other two were with a private business that had a contract with the sheriff's department. Still, there was nothing illegal about flying a drone to his island. He would clean the machine up, reprogram it, and use it at work for one of his projects. More importantly, he was now on high alert as it seemed that Sheriff Wendy Knight planned to take him down.

He dropped a note to the chief and DA notifying them of what happened, and the identities of the involved parties for their records. He also said that his island was in no danger and that he had confiscated the drone for use in his business.

Both parties asked Damian if he was safe and speculated about what to do with the men involved in the launch. Damian recommended doing nothing at the moment. It was better to know who one's enemies were than to fire the enemy's minions. It would be easy to get distracted by chasing around many small parties attached to their suspect rather than going after the big cheese. In the end, he might have a nice collection of drones if another attempt was made to survey his island. He could operate his defensive systems remotely and could take down any unwelcome visitors when he was away from the island.

Damian had given some thought to his work location, and while he didn't have the same security there, his company wasn't registered in his name and his vehicle was registered to the company, so again, he would be hard to find unless he was followed from the Richmond marina. He also had cameras on Ariana's house and would know if the sheriff's goons connected her to him. He returned to the video footage to understand how much of his island was photographed by the drone before its demise. Would they plan an attack after dark if they knew the layout?

The sheriff would be foolish if she did that. His island had been attacked before by a prison gang and he defended it well. Whatever group Sheriff Knight sent would be less of a problem. Still, when he went to bed, he made doubly sure that the island was locked up tight and the alarms set so he would have advance warning of any approaching hostiles.

Around one in the morning, the alarm sounded on his phone, waking him up. Using the phone flashlight feature, he went down to his lab to prepare to defend the island. First, he needed to see what was up. In theory, someone could have a motor failure and drift toward the boundary of his alarms, but in his ten years on the island, that had yet to happen.

He opened his alarm system to see what had triggered it. A boat was approaching the narrow beach. Local maps of the area, unfortunately, featured his island, so someone could decide to try to reach his house by landing on the beach first. They would have a rocky hillside to climb in the dark, but his visitors would soon find the error of their ways.

Damian watched the boat get closer and prepared to bombard it with the water cannons he had built into the hillside. He had an unlimited supply of pressurized cold bay water to aim at the unwelcome visitors. He watched the boat's approach just to make sure it wasn't in distress. He saw the heat signatures of three humans and an engine that was working. Yes, they were unfriendlies. He launched his drone from the other side of the island preparing to drop dye on them. He liked to mark any trespassers with a bright green dye that would take between ten and twenty baths to eliminate. He also had audio alarms and bright lights he could focus on the boat, but he preferred hitting them with the water and dye in the dark as they would be caught unaware. The advantage of living on your own island was you didn't worry about annoying your neighbors with noise or light.

Ten minutes later he briefly smiled as he watched the boat leave the island's perimeter heading back toward wherever it was docked. He recorded the entire episode on tape. Sadly, in the low visibility light, he was unable to identify the men. Damian made a mess of them and their boat. His drones had pelted the men and their boat with balloons filled with lime-green dye. There was a heated conversation that he couldn't hear, but he could tell they were unhappy. So he opened his water cannons next, which blasted the men to the floor of the boat while one of them tried to turn the boat around and head away from the island and out of range of the water. He sent the video to the chief and DA with a summary and returned to his bed. At least tomorrow he would get a good night's sleep in Carmel; then again, the fools might attack his island a second night in a row, and he would have to defend it remotely from afar, which was harder to do.

Later that morning, he was on a video call with the committee. The chief asked him to play the video footage for the group of both the drone and the early morning boat. A few people in the room laughed and clapped when the dye and water hit the men.

"Damian, besides your extraordinary computer skills, I must

say that your home defense system makes you a perfect member of this committee. In your place, I would have been intimidated and be making calls to get a helicopter out to the island. Instead, you're a one-man wrecking ball for anyone who dares to step on your island without your approval," an attorney representing the county said. "In fact, can I pay you to install a similar system at my house?"

"You don't have the unlimited supply of bay water that I do, so it wouldn't work. I can give you the recipe to make the green dye and the model of a drone if you would like to drop dye on any burglars that approach your property."

"I'd appreciate the recipe and the drone model."

"As I like to promote nonviolent means of self-defense, I'll distribute Mr. Green's recipe and model number to members of this committee," the chief said. "Moving on to an update on this case: We have a series of suspicious financial transactions, but we don't have a strong connection to Wendy Knight personally. Our DA states that there isn't enough to prosecute at this stage. So I wanted to use this session to brainstorm what other pieces of information we could use to prove a corruption charge against the sheriff. Damian was able to locate the offshore and dark web transfers of money. The problem is that we can see the movement of funds, but we can't see that Sheriff Knight was behind any of those actions. I'd like to bring a forensic accountant on board and have them work with county counsel and Damian to find precise money movement that can be traced to our suspect."

Damian watched as people nodded and then asked the question he hadn't heard answered.

"Can you give me the names of the people who have disappeared? I'd like to trace them. Isn't it better to convict her for murder than illegal financial transactions?"

"She'll serve a longer sentence if she is linked to a murder. My observation of her is that she doesn't do her own dirty work. However, conspiracy to commit murder will lock her up for a while, and I hadn't meant to ignore our missing witnesses. I'll have Natalie share those missing-person cases with you. The sheriff is up for re-election in six months so it would be nice if we collected clear and convicting evidence soon. Her name won't be removed from the ballot, but at least people will have that information when they vote." replied Chief Swanson. He appeared to be a mixed-race tall man in his early fifties. He had a voice that would make most mild criminals rethink their plans.

"Great. I'll sign off now and go to work on the items you need. I'll also send you the plan for the drone defense system."

"Thank you for your time, Mr. Green, and let us know if there is any way we can assist you in staying safe," Chief Swanson said.

Damian nodded and ended the video call. He needed to visit his company today and then he would start on the computer information the committee was looking for. He wondered if the sheriff had hired someone to follow him. Given that his island was attacked, it was likely that the sheriff might have a tail on him at the Richmond dock. He'd bring a device with him to see if there were any trackers on his vehicles and advise Ariana to do likewise with the device he'd left at her house after a stalker entered her life. A quick text to her and he was in his boat on his way to the marina.

He reached his truck in the marina parking lot to find two flat tires. He noticed two men walking toward him. In his ten years of building a house and then living on Red Rock Island, he'd never been approached by strangers in the marina parking lot. He thought they were likely minions of the sheriff. He debated how close he wanted them to get and he decided the answer was not close at all.

He had a variety of options to deal with them at the ready as he'd expected trouble when he left his island. He didn't know if they were armed, but they could have guns tucked in their pants in the back. He quickly decided on a strategy based on the fact that no one else was near him.

He pulled out a homemade potassium perchlorate and aluminum powder grenade better known as a flash-bang. Since his grenade was homemade, he added chemical coloring to make the smoke denser so it would emit a colorful pink smoke. After tossing it in the direction of the two men, he moved to the side and threw a second bomb to further distract them while he headed back to the dock to return to his boat. He was tempted to return with a water gun he had filled with a vinegar mixture but decided it was better to disengage and find another marina. He knew multiple places he could dock his boat on the east side of San Francisco Bay. He would have his tires repaired and move his truck to a safer location until this investigation was over.

He backed his boat away from the dock and headed south toward Berkeley. There were at least three other marinas that were closer, but he figured his suspicious men would look there first. At least their clothes would be stained from the dye in his smoke bomb, so they would have to discard their clothing. Their hair would also be stained, but the dye would wash out after ten or so shampoos. At least if they came after him in the next week or so, he would recognize them by their lime-green or pink hair depending on where they had interacted with him. That thought made him smile.

He tied up his boat in a slip and covered it in case the men chasing him had a description of it. He was soon taking a rideshare car to his warehouse in Richmond. He hoped the men wouldn't be there when he arrived. He asked one of his employees to check the parking lot and it was clear at the moment. Seconds after he arrived, he was carded through the front door of his warehouse and on the way up to his second-floor office. He decided that he needed to put his employees on alert as this had rapidly become a dangerous situation. Of course, it wasn't the first one he and his employees had experienced. He had on other occasions moved their office to his island, but he didn't think he was there in this scenario.

He normally held an all-staff meeting on Fridays to talk about projects. This time they would have a little more to chat about. Half an hour later, he explained his latest project for the police.

"How do you end up with the dregs of society after you? You would think that being a computer geek doing a few random data runs would fail to be noticed by most criminals," Haley said. She was married to Retired Detective Natalie Severino's son, Trevor, who was an assistant district attorney in a nearby county.

"It's probably my fault. When your mother-in-law first asked me to join the case at the request of her police chief, I likely made everyone mad in the video call when I told them I would be investigating them first and asked them to spell their full names for me. Maybe I shouldn't have specified my intentions and instead quietly investigated everyone."

"Was anyone on the committee a crook?"

"Yes. A county supervisor had some illegal payments made to him offshore and inside the dark web. That person was removed from the committee investigating the sheriff, so they knew that I was responsible for finding the information they thought was deeply buried."

"Yeah, Damian!" Lily said. She was an ex-bank robber and a mathematical whiz. "If you need any help searching for more financial transactions, let me know. I can work on it over the weekend. Jacob is away for a basketball camp so I have time on my hands and would love to help you bring down crooked politicians." Jacob was her fourteen-year-old son.

"I might take you up on that idea, Lily. Ariana, Hermione, and I are going to Carmel for the weekend. Hermione is driving both ways to get part of her student driving requirements fulfilled, but I won't have much time to work on stuff. The DA wants more direct links from the sheriff to a variety of funds. I'll give you some more information on it and maybe you'll find something."

"Given your truck's flat tires, is it safe for Hermione to drive with you in the car until this case is resolved?" Chris asked.

"I hadn't thought of that. Crap! Maybe not, or maybe I'll start out driving and turn the car over to her after I take a few on and off-ramps to make sure no one is following us. My only connection to Ariana and Hermione is on her school registration."

"I thought Ariana was listed as the COO of this company?"

"This morning, is seems that all of my employees are smarter than me. You're right, Chris. Aarrgghh."

"You're a little slow this morning because you were woken up in the middle of the night and had to defend your castle. That was followed by some more self-defense against two goons who might have kidnapped you. And that was all before lunch," Haley said.

"You're too kind. I think I'll arrange to have my tires repaired and then I'll store the truck in a storage facility that I have until this case is over. I'll just have to plan to dock at different marinas around the area and take a rideshare to work. All this aggravation makes me want to work harder to bring down this corrupt sheriff. She has met her match in me. I'll fight her corruption with my giant computers and her bullets with my homemade smoke bombs and pepper spray. She is going down," Damian said, his voice brimming with determination.

He was startled by a round of applause from his employees and that made him smile. It felt good to have friends on his side. He knew the police chief and the DA supported him, but that didn't mean they stood in front of him to take any bullets flying his way. They would probably rather put them in protective custody and hope the sheriff couldn't breach their designated safe house. He'd take his chances on defending his island, his business, his family, and his employees.

He moved the group beyond his own problems to their weekly update on where they were with the various technologies. Haley was working on a drone project for him, and he could see how he could use her latest tweaks to better defend himself even though that wasn't the purpose of her project.

They all went downstairs to Pete's restaurant for lunch before returning to the office to get more work done. Lily dropped Damian at the marina and he journeyed back to his island to get ready for their weekend in Carmel. He rented a small house close to the beach. Carmel was a very dog-friendly town and so Miguel, Ariana's Portuguese water dog, was joining them on this trip.

# CHAPTER 4

After he reached Ariana's dock on the other side of the bay, he locked up the boat and carried his overnight bag to Ariana's SUV. Her house was located in the city of Belvedere, which was northeast of the Golden Gate Bridge. Her house was on the water and was a modern two-story with a pool where they taught Hermione the game of water polo and practiced scuba diving. He scanned the vehicle and found no tracking devices. He also brought a bag of self-defense items in case the sheriff's department caught up to him. Normally, he would travel through Santa Clara County to reach Carmel, but given that he had a target on his back, he was taking the longer route via Highway One down the coast.

"Are you sure I can't drive the entire way to Carmel?" Hermione asked.

"I would be an irresponsible parent to put an inexperienced driver such as yourself behind the wheel knowing that someone is out to get me. After you have more hours driving or you've graduated from an evasive driving course, then I'd let you drive."

"They have evasive driving classes?"

"Yes. If you're on the security detail for an important person, then you have to be ready for bad actors to come at you when you're on the road."

"Maybe after I've been driving for a year or so, we could all take a course like that? You seem to make a lot of enemies, Damian, and it often spills over to Ariana and me. Seems like we would all benefit from a class as you described."

"Kiddo, sadly, I think you're right. Though to be fair, we've had bad people come after you and Ariana almost as much as me. From what I've seen, Hermione, you're very cool under pressure and that's half the battle for evasive driving."

While they were having this conversation, they loaded the car with their luggage, cooler, dog stuff, and Damian's bag of tricks. They entered the car, buckled up, and headed up the driveway. Damian studied the cars on the street and didn't see anything that concerned him. He wound his way through the little hamlet of Belvedere and toward Highway 101, which would take him across the Golden Gate Bridge. There was silence in the car as they all stared at the cars around them trying to determine if any of them were following them. It was hard to tell as traffic was typically busy on a Friday evening. After the bridge, a three-lane road in each direction took them through the San Francisco Presidio and onto a freeway. In the suburb of Scrramontc, thcy got off the freeway and followed the two-lane highway down the coast. They would get most of the way in daylight and so could delight in the views of the Pacific Ocean. After they cleared the bustle of San Francisco and the worry of someone following them, conversation resumed in the car.

"Did you do anything with the data I sent you on the track and field events?" Damian asked Hermione.

"Yeah. I shared it with the coach, and she had me exclusively work on thc high hurdles and the long jump. I'm not the best at either yet, but I have three months to work on them before regional finals."

"Instead of having the goal of reaching regional finals, perhaps you might have the goal of gaining inches in the long jump or cutting time off your hurdles," Ariana suggested.

"You know me—go big or go home."

"You know, you might be mediocre at these track events. It's really hard to be the top dog in everything you try."

"Kiddo, you're spoiled by the success that is coming easily to you in school and athletics. That's great that you don't have to struggle, but I worry about the first time you fail at something," Damian said.

"What have you failed at, Damian?" Hermione asked.

"The biggest failure of all—I didn't save my family from being victims of random violence." His wife and two girls were murdered by a parolee who decided he wanted his wife's car to use as an escape vehicle. She gave the convict the keys and yet he still shot them dead. It had all been captured on their home security system. Natalie was the detective who cornered the convict and she had shot him dead in self-defense.

There was dead silence in the car, as none of them knew the right words to say to Damian regarding the loss of his family from a mistakenly released prisoner.

After a while, Hermione ventured to ask, "What could you have done differently that day?"

"If I'm honest with myself, nothing at all. However, I keep a database on all criminals convicted of felonies to make sure there are no more accidental releases of horrible human beings from any prison."

Hermione and Ariana each put a hand on Damian in comfort as they had no words to say to the sudden dark and sad direction their conversation had taken. A short time later, Damian was slowing down to pull over.

"I've been studying the rearview mirror and I haven't seen anyone following us, so I'm turning the car over to you," Damian said to Hermione.

"Yay!" Hermione said, and they all switched places in the car.

Hermione took the driver's seat; Damian took the front passenger seat and Ariana moved to the back. Thus far, Hermione had received all her driving instructions from Ariana. It would be good for Damian to provide supervision.

The teenager got in, put her seatbelt on, adjusted the mirrors, and looked over her shoulder to pull onto the road. The view of the ocean was spectacular; they were just north of Half Moon Bay where once a year, the Mavericks surf contest took place. Each winter the surf produced waves up to sixty feet high, and it was a magnificent sight to watch. Damian had been tempted to open the sunroof to listen to the waves, but he didn't want Hermione to be distracted by the sound. Also, he would need to focus on his surroundings until his case with the sheriff was closed.

As they were approaching Santa Cruz, dusk was falling and Damian asked, "Are you allowed to drive in the dark with your learner's permit?"

"Yes. I can't drive after 11pm or before 5am, but we should be to Carmel by then, right?"

"Yes. Okay then, let's be careful with the busy beach traffic of Santa Cruz."

"I will. Can we talk about something while I'm driving? My eyes are glued to the road, but the silence in this car is a distraction. Tell me about work or your latest cop case. I noticed you used the wand on Ariana's car before we left, so you must be in trouble in one of those areas."

"Kiddo, sometimes you're too smart and observant for your own good. I guess I shouldn't worry about your driving. My latest cop case as you call it is a doozy. There's a corrupt elected sheriff that the police and district attorney want my help to expose her misdeeds before her election six months from now."

"That sounds like a lot of time for you to find evidence and it's not a cold case, is it?"

"You're correct. I don't want to become a regular detective of the police department even though they have offered me a full-time job, but I hate corruption of any sort and she's got quite a racket going on."

"Has she come after you?" Hermione asked with curiosity rather than worry in her voice.

"Yes. I was brought into a 'secret committee' that wasn't secret. I started by investigating everyone on the committee and told them upfront I would do so. I discovered one of the county supervisors on the committee had a payoff in his bank account that the DA and chief didn't find when they vetted the committee members. He was bounced from the committee, so the sheriff no longer knows what is going on with the investigation."

"So she knows who you are and thinks she has reason to go after you."

"Yes, that was a mistake on my part. I should have handled it differently at the start, but I let my temper get the better of me."

"She would have found out who you were eventually, though. Better to not be caught unaware. Did she have someone attack you?"

"Kiddo, sometimes you're so smart in reasoning through people's motives that you scare me. Last night while I was fishing for the cats I heard a drone heading my way. I downed it with oil and disconnected the battery. I gave it to Haley to use at work as it was a nice model given that it could reach my house from the shore. Then I was woken by three men in a boat who tried to breach my island."

"Did you hit them with the water cannons?"

"I did and also dropped the green dye balloons. They departed after the shower in the dark. When I got to the marina this morning, my truck had two flat tires and two men tried to approach me. I tossed a few smoke bombs at them, retreated to my boat, and went south to another marina and on to the office."

"No wonder you were scanning cars around us! You've had a busy twenty-four hours," Ariana said.

"It's also why we're taking the longer route south as I'm

staying out of the sheriff's territory. I don't know if she knows about you, but if this car is followed at some point, then we'll have to take precautions with you and Hermione. I might have to move you over to the island," Damian said.

"That would be inconvenient, but I understand. Better to be safe."

"Yeah, other people involved with digging up information on her have disappeared off the face of the earth so I'm trying to track them down. It was why I tossed smoke bombs at the two men that approached me today. I didn't know if they were armed, and it wasn't safe for me to find out. They didn't visit the warehouse while I was there so hopefully, that stays a secret. I can keep coming ashore at one of the ten or so marinas lining the east bay."

Damian felt Ariana's hand on his shoulder. He reached up and covered her hand with his.

"Maybe we should have stayed home," Hermione said.

"I admit I thought about doing that, but I think we'll be okay by staying out on the coast rather than going inland, which is a faster drive. She has her tentacles in many areas as evidenced by her men coming to my island and my parking lot, but I can't let her paralyze me with fear. That said, I have a bag of tricks packed in case her people try to catch my attention while we're in Carmel."

Hermione negotiated the Santa Cruz traffic, and they were averaging forty miles per hour heading south toward Moss Landing. A travel app said the road would be getting a little faster and they had about half an hour to reach Carmel. After finding their lodging and unloading supplies, they headed toward a restaurant that would allow Miguel to join them. Doris Day had been a Carmel resident, a staunch supporter of the Humane Society, and the reason that dogs were welcomed in as many places as the Health Department allowed in the city.

They were seated and awaiting their food when Hermione

asked Damian, "How did you like my driving? You didn't say much on the road."

"I didn't say much as you are an excellent driver. I think you have an innate core of self-sufficiency that keeps you alive in difficult circumstances. You kept your eyes on the road and were aware of the drivers around you. That's all you can do to drive well and avoid other, stupid drivers. You also kept your speed close to the limit. That's hard to do with people whipping past you and you'll probably drive like that one day. At this time in your life, you shouldn't be speeding."

"That was sort of my thinking on the subject. I knew I could get us here faster, but it was not worth what being stopped by a cop would do to my student driving record."

"Once you have your license next year, we'll get you a small electric vehicle. At your age, you shouldn't be driving far, so the short range of an electric vehicle suits you. Even when you're a student at Berkeley, that car should serve you, though you won't need one on campus."

Hermione proceeded to reel off the name and features of the car she wanted, and Damian couldn't disagree with her choices.

"I'm glad you said I should have an electric car. That's better for the environment," Hermione said.

"I might make it ugly by modifying it with some solar panels and an extra battery unit."

"I'm sure that whatever you design, it will be pretty and my classmates will be jealous."

"Wow, that is such praise from a teenager."

"On that note, is anyone interested in dessert?" Ariana asked, eyeing the menu. They had finished their meals while discussing driving. When the three of them were together, she tended to drift off during the conversations between Hermione and Damian. She was with the teenager all week and got a lot more quality time with their ward than he did.

"Yes, I ran and jumped a lot today, so I need dessert. Let me see," Hermione said putting her hand out to receive the menu from Ariana.

"Kiddo, I'm with you. I'm sure I burned a lot of calories fighting off the men attacking my island and me at my truck."

"I don't have room for dessert, but I'll have a taste of each of your choices," Ariana said.

It was the start of a relaxing weekend in the quaint coastal city of Carmel. Despite the fact they were only an hour away from the corrupt sheriff's jurisdiction, it was far enough to feel safe and not worry about her and her co-conspirators.

Damian briefly weighed taking the shorter route home through the sheriff's county, but he decided to play it safe and stay on the coast while heading north toward San Francisco and beyond. Hermione was again at the wheel, with Ariana in the front and Damian in the back. He could still converse with the teenager when he needed to, but he felt freer to study the cars around them as they made the journey home. Traffic was heavy in sections as people traveled home for the work week. They would make it to San Francisco before it turned dark, and Damian expected good light for him to examine the cars around them. They reached a deserted section north of Half Moon Bay and something caught Damian's attention. He was soon sorting through his bag of weapons and assessing what to do with Hermione at the wheel. If someone was truly evil, they could side-swipe Ariana's SUV and attempt to send them over the cliff to the Pacific Ocean.

His ever-alert teenager realized that something was up. She must have been watching her side and rear-view mirrors. "Should I pull over?"

"No. I may have you slow your speed and open the sunroof. I have some things to toss at that car and I just need to think about the physics of how to do it best."

"Give me something I can lob at that car," Ariana said.

Damian was worried because there were other cars on the

road. There weren't many, but chances were that if he had Hermione slow the car down, traffic would back up behind them and anything he threw at the car that was pursuing them might impact those behind it. Furthermore, what if he was wrong? What if the car didn't contain a person meaning to do the three of them harm? He did a quick search of the car's license plate and of the registered owner. It was a former deputy sheriff from Sheriff Knight's department.

"Okay, I just verified that vehicle belongs to one of the corrupt sheriff's minions. What are the odds of that person randomly following us on a Sunday afternoon?" Damian asked of the car's occupants.

"Nada," Hermione said.

"Zip," Ariana added.

"I'm glad you ladies agree with me. Now the trick is going to be how to slow their car down without taking anyone else with them."

"I could greatly speed up and that car would also have to do so to keep pace with us, then I could slow down quickly and the two of you could lob whatever surprises you have. There isn't much traffic coming from the opposite direction," Hermione suggested.

"Those are good suggestions. Our other choice would be to turn off this road. We would have solid proof that they were following us and if we damage their car and force them off the road, it won't hurt any other drivers in the vicinity," Damian said.

"I like your suggestion, Damian. In particular, we would have to slow down a lot to turn onto another street and that would give you and me a better chance at throwing stuff."

"Let me know when you're ready with lots of things to lob at that car and I'll turn at the next street," Hermione said.

Damian quickly distributed things to throw to Ariana and looked for her nod of readiness.

"We're ready. You're doing a great job of staying steady at the wheel, Kiddo."

"Thanks. Too bad I can't get bonus hours for driving under stressful situations. There's a street coming up that looks perfect. I'm going to turn soon onto Sunnybeach Road, according to the sign."

"Open the sunroof. I'll use it as I'm in a better position to stand," Ariana said.

Hermione hit the sunroof button as she began slowing down to make the turn. Damian put his window down on the right side of the car, ready to pitch like it was the World Series. Ariana stood up through the sunroof just as the car made the turn. Hermione stayed at a slow speed even after they had turned.

All three of them noted that the car followed them onto the new road. Ariana waited for the car to get closer and tossed her first balloon at the car. She felt the weight of it and did her own calculus of time, distance, and speed, and scored a bullseye on the car windshield smearing it with a black tar-like substance. The driver immediately made his situation worse by smearing the substance with his wiper washers. While the driver was distracted by his windshield, Damian threw handfuls of spikes shaped like jacks all over the road. His jacks were made from titanium and had very sharp points. The tires of the chasing vehicle would be going flat soon. The driver was leaning out his side of the car, trying to raise a gun in their direction.

"Try to weave the car a little. The jerk has a gun and that will make it harder for the driver to hit us," Damian said. "Hermione, sit low in your seat."

He immediately felt the car swaying and hoped it would buy them some time. It helped that the driver had to lean out of his car since the windshield was a smeary mess. Most people were right-handed and that hopefully meant that the driver was firing with his nondominant hand. The driver was having a hard time balancing driving, leaning out a window to see where the road was, and getting his arm into a shooting stance.

Damian heard the sound of a gun being fired and looked

around the car to make sure that Ariana and Hermione were okay. When he turned his attention back to the car, he saw that his jacks had worked, as it appeared there were two tires quickly deflating.

"Round two to the good guys," Damian said, pumping his arms as he watched the car slow behind them. He wouldn't be going anywhere soon, and they would soon be out of range unless he was a sniper; but by the time the driver stopped, got out of his car, set up a sniper rifle, and focused, they would be out of his range.

Ariana sat down in her seat, buckled her seatbelt, and said, "We appear to be in the clear. I think his tire went flat just as he fired, so the car wasn't hit. Should we call the police?"

"I'm going to call the chief in San Jose and notify him even though this isn't his jurisdiction. I don't know who we can trust in neighboring police forces not to be friends with Sheriff Knight. Besides, someone needs to pick up the jacks I dropped on the road, otherwise there will be lots of flat tires."

"Before you do that, can someone direct me out of here? I don't know where this road goes, but we're heading east instead of north," Hermione said.

"Do you need someone else to drive?" Ariana asked, concerned about the teenager's nerves. She was very resilient, but still, these past ten minutes had been very difficult for an experienced driver let alone one who was still a student driver.

"I'm good. Just give me directions." Ariana squeezed her arm and said, "Just a minute while I pull up my driving app."

Damian checked on the two important women in his life and decided things were under control. He called the chief, summarized what happened, and the problem with the road.

"I wonder how someone found you. You're not in your vehicle, and you went south to a county well beyond Sheriff Knight's. She has quite an empire if she has the manpower to locate you in Monterey County."

"Chief, I've been wondering that myself. We stayed in a rental, so we weren't on the radar of any hotel databases. We watched on our way out of the city to see if anyone was following us and didn't find anything. We were left alone in Carmel. The car we're traveling in is registered to a friend. When I return to my home, I'm going to find out where I tripped up. Somehow, she knew I wasn't home on the island, as it wasn't attacked over the weekend."

"Let me know what you find. I'll let a friend in the San Mateo sheriff's department know about the damage to the road. I could try and have the driver arrested, but this is a 'he said, she said' situation. I'd rather take care of it later when we have a full list of activities that the sheriff directed. Would you agree?"

"Yes, we didn't get anything on film. Talk to you later." Damian ended the call with the chief.

"Everyone okay? Do we know where we are going?" Damian asked.

"Yes, and yes," Hermione said, while Ariana leaned on the center armrest, looked back, and nodded. "I have navigation taking us through these hills. Hopefully, we'll have cellular reception the entire way. We should pop out back to Highway 280 with a few more turns."

"Awesome. As partners in crime, you two ladies always exceed my expectation in fighting off bad guys."

"It's only because you carry a strange bag of tricks with you wherever we go," Ariana said.

"Yes, but where would we be without your pitch of my tar balloon to disable the man's windshield?" Damian said. "I'm going to do more research to figure out how our suspect found us in Carmel. I think when we get home, you should park this car in the garage and get a rental car. Likewise, I'm putting my truck in storage until this case is over."

"I have a friend I'll swap cars with," Ariana said.

"I'd advise that you not do that as many of the sheriff's coons don't know what you look like and you might put your friend at risk."

"Of course, you're right. Why don't we detour right now to the airport? I'll get a rental and you can follow me to my start-up biotech company, which is close by. I'll notify building security that the car is going to sit there for a few days."

"I think this case is going to go longer than some of our other cases with bad dudes. The DA has to have all his ducks in order if he wants to arrest the sheriff. I'm sure that arresting her and later convicting her is the only thing that will stop the attacks from coming our way. At least if she was in jail, it would stop her communication with her goons. Are you sure you want to leave your car at the biotech company for potentially as long as a month?"

"If they know I'm connected to you, and they know what I drive, then they know my home address. Maybe I'll rent a boat dock at the Sausalito marina and park my rental car there. I could then take my boat to the marina and pick my car up there. I can work out an arrangement with the other parents or with a rideshare driver to get Hermione to school."

"I know that's really inconvenient, ladies, but I would feel better with you taking precautions. We seem to have a fair number of bad law enforcement agents. Normally we would feel relieved if we saw their badge, but in this situation, it's not good. I can't imagine that she has contacts in the Belvedere police department. So maybe we can let them in on the situation?"

"I see signs for the airport. Do you want me to head into it and follow the signs for the rental cars?" Hermione asked.

"Yes, please. You are brilliant, Kiddo."

"Okay, I'll go in and rent a car for a month and then you two can follow me to Sausalito and I'll see about renting a boat slip and car space there for the month. When I need to leave Belvedere, I'll take my pontoon boat over there. Even if someone is watching me, they can't get over to Sausalito fast enough to track me. I'll think of some more precautions I can take," Ariana said.

Hermione parked the car and the three of them walked into the rental agency.

"Can I just say how much I appreciate the lack of drama about how this situation is affecting you ladies? I'm sorry that my work assisting the SJPD is impacting your routines and putting your lives in danger," Damian said.

"No worries. We'll get through this crisis just as we have the other ones. We've got your back, don't we, Hermione?" Ariana said in cheerleading mode. She kept pushing her short black hair behind her ear. That was the trouble with bobs—the hair was long enough to cover your eyes.

"You bet. I had the best driving experience tonight. It was something I'll never be taught in school, but once I begin driving by myself, I think I'd like to have a bag of your jacks in the car with me in case someone bothers me. Of course, that's in addition to my water gun filled with eye-burning acid," Hermione said.

"The world is full of good people, and once you go to college, I can't imagine any bad people chasing me also going after you on your college campus. So just a few more years of dealing with these idiots who think they can escape the long arm of the law by taking us out of the picture. We have better, nonviolent means to keep the baddies away."

"My life is so weird, I'm not sure how I would explain it to anyone. I'll need to go to college with the name Hermione Knowles as that will match my high school transcripts. I guess I'm Hermione for the rest of my life. It's a good thing I like the name."

"If it makes you feel any better, all of our lives are weird," Ariana said with a smile.

# CHAPTER 5

*D*amian had been late returning to his home on the island the previous night. There had been a lot of work to do to arrange the slip and parking space for Ariana in Sausalito. He made sure the alarms were set at her house and the few weapons around the exterior were in working order. He'd hugged the ladies goodbye and traveled the short commute to his island on his speed boat. He thought about getting some sleep, but the risks the sheriff put him through with his ward and girlfriend angered him. It was one thing to come after him, but nothing would make him put more effort into bringing the sheriff down than going after his family. He lost one family to a criminal; he wasn't going to lose a second time. He also wondered how the sheriff had tracked them from Carmel to home.

He stared at the wall in his computer lab and thought about the evidence he needed to gather to send Sheriff Wendy Knight to jail for a long time. He debated whether to work on the other people who disappeared and try to link those missing persons to her or do a lengthy deep dive into her financial transactions. From what the chief said, she had a fifteen- to twenty-year history of bribery, corruption, and who knew what other crimes.

Damian began researching other law enforcement leaders who took a wrong turn. He started with some historical stories from the 1920s forward. How these leaders did bad things before technology wouldn't be helpful, but maybe it would help him understand the psyche of those who went astray.

Two hours later, he was thoroughly depressed. It was a case of absolute power corrupts absolutely, a quote by Lord Acton. He then distracted himself further by reading up on Lord Acton. Basically, the problem was as elected sheriffs, these law enforcement types were accountable to the voters, and that happened only every four years during an election. Many elected sheriffs operated the prison located in their jurisdiction. People died in prison from fights and beatings. He wouldn't have minded that happening to the criminal who had murdered his family, but often people in jails that the sheriffs managed were pre-trial or had short sentences for nonviolent crimes. Those people didn't deserve to die.

In other regions, the sheriff was responsible for unincorporated areas or sometimes contracted with a city to be its police force. There were stories about speed traps, confiscation of cars, and drugs (legal and illegal) that were sold for cash for the department. Some sheriffs specialized in hiring deputies who were convicted of a criminal act while on duty in another department. One sheriff of a large department was rumored to have created gangs within his workforce. His local corrupt sheriff seemed to give these other abusive sheriffs a run for their money on the question of who was the worse. Sheriff Wendy Knight had unexpected deaths among her custody inmates, her staff were noted for taking bribes, and she handed out concealed carry permits to gun owners who contributed to her reelection campaign. Normally, the permits were hard to obtain as an applicant had to prove *good cause*, but this allowed the sheriff to apply her discretion as to who she approved for the permit.

What he also learned in reading these past histories of corrupt sheriffs was that they routinely got away with their criminal behavior, often retiring on a nice monthly pension. Well, he was going to do his best to find evidence for the DA to charge her, which hopefully would also impact her pension. With this last thought, he decided he was ready to retire for the night. He had a full day planned later this morning including finding alternate places to dock his boat on the east side of the bay.

He also had a thought charge cross his mind—burner phones. He bet the sheriff was tracking him by following his cell phone signal. Unfortunately, his phone had spent time in the vicinity of Ariana and the dock in Sausalito, and at SFO. To track his cell phone someone would've had to have gotten a court order and that meant the sheriff had a judge in her pocket too. If the sheriff's goons got a list of all his calls, they would soon know Ariana's and Hermione's phone numbers. He sent a text to Ariana asking her to get hold of anonymous phones at nearby stores that carried such items. A new phone wouldn't have all the bells and whistles of the smartphone, but at least their movements wouldn't be tracked. What a pain this case was becoming, and he couldn't help wondering what would've happened if the man following them yesterday had them alone with the gun. Would he have murdered three people in cold blood?

After a quick but restful sleep, Damian approached the day with determination. He docked his boat in the San Pablo Marina, north of where he usually docked. He arranged a car service to pick him up and stop at a store to buy a phone. He then pulled the SIM card out of his existing phone, which would prevent all tracking. He called Ariana and Hermione to give them his new number knowing his call would go to voicemail as the number was unrecognizable to the two of them. He also reminded them that he would be at the office and they could reach him there if they had any issues. When he reached his warehouse, he gathered his employees around to inform them of the latest developments with his case.

"Boss, I think you should play some games with the SIM card," Angus said. "I think you should have the phone move around unconnected to yourself. For example, you could mail the phone somewhere in the world. You could expand Haley's project with drones and have her move the phone around that way. I could probably locate some scary houses containing ex-convicts who are gang members. Haley could drop the phone on the roof of the house for a few hours. Let's see if your corrupt sheriff sends some of her idiot followers to those locations."

"Wow, Angus, those are brilliant suggestions. I should have thought of them myself. Haley, do you think you could do as Angus suggests?"

"Probably. It's a good idea to further my testing with the drone. However, instead of using your fancy smartphone, can you get a burner or at least an old smartphone and put the SIM card in that? That way, if it's forever lost on some horrible person's roof, I won't feel bad."

"That's another brilliant idea from a staff member! Thanks, Haley. What kind of range does your drone have?" Damian asked.

"It has tested for five miles and I'm working on seven miles. I could move boxes for you from the Richmond marina to your island."

"Angus, give me some addresses of horrible neighbors and I'll find a smartphone to dump on a roof. I'd like to leave it overnight, so they're tempted to raid the location. I'll need to charge it fully and keep the phone on silent, so it doesn't ring on the roof. I think I'll also have to pass on to the police chief and DA my new phone number and the concept that the sheriff has a judge in her pocket in order to be able to track a private citizen's phone. Do you guys have any other ideas that I can use to protect myself, my, home, Ariana and Hermione, or this building?"

"I could add some drones to our roof here. The trouble is that we must decide who is coming for a meal at Pete's restaurant and who is a dirty cop intent on harming us," Haley said.

"I've got a software program that I've been working on that might help. It uses some of the same technology as security scanners at the airport, so it should be able to identify if someone has a gun or other weapon on them. That will isolate the hostiles," Chris said.

"Hostiles?" Damian asked with a bemused grin. He was awed by his employees' suggestions on how to improve their security.

"I've been watching too many thriller movies at night," Chris said with a shrug.

"Can you demo your system? I'll walk across the parking lot with a water gun and a knife, and we'll see what it picks up. I'd like to take a variety of knives—a switchblade, a bowie or kitchen knife, and a Swiss army knife. I'm not sure how many people carry Swiss army knives on them routinely and we could end up acid washing a loyal customer of Pete's," Damian said.

"Yes, that would be bad," Lily agreed. "Is there a technology the sheriff might use that would decipher whether you're in residence on your island?"

"Thermal imaging can work for quite some distance including standing in Richmond and sensing your heat on the island. However, your lower level is built into the rock, and I thought you wrapped the house in a special metal that would repel a thermal imaging camera," Chris said.

"Chris is correct. My home's construction should prevent the use of thermal imaging. A drone cannot see into the house. However thermal imaging would be able to detect people at Ariana's house. If I move them to my house, I'll need to supply her with a boat that fits in my watercraft garage, and it becomes a pain to get Hermione to school. I have security on her house in terms of sensors and acid spray on the driveway. However, the dock has just a water spray. Suggestions?"

"Do you have reason to think the sheriff will go after them?" Angus asked. "Have you looked into the family and friends of the other people who disappeared to see if there were any issues?"

"I haven't. Once we're done here, I'll immediately look at that. I'd rather not have to worry about the two of them. Well, I should restate that—I always worry about them. I would rather not worry about them in regard to this sheriff's goons. Hermione needs to go to school and she's training for the track and field team and there are meets coming up. Their lives are more complicated than mine."

"I would think that the judge who signed off on the order to track your phone would also have to provide a court order to track Ariana and Hermione, but the order for those phone numbers would have come a few days after your court order. Perhaps you should mail the phones to someone in Southern California and have them leave the phones at, say, the Coronado Island Resort. That way it will look like they are on vacation. Some of her goons must be dumber and dumber, so that will keep them busy for a while. Also, could you call your friends at the FBI and have them counterorder the phone company?" Haley suggested.

"Good suggestions, Haley. I think I will call the FBI. I don't know that they can do anything, but it's worth a try. On another note, is anything we're talking about capable of being commercialized?" Damian asked with a smile.

"Trust you to have your brain working in multiple directions at the same time," Chris said as the team laughed with Damian.

"Thanks, team, for listening and brainstorming. I like your devious minds' suggestions on how to make life difficult for the bad sheriff's goons."

"Since I served time for a crime I didn't commit thanks to bad police work, I'll be willing to devote all of my spare time to catching this piece of human trash," Angus said.

"Thanks, I appreciate the offer, Angus I'll . . .," Damian was cut off by Chris, Haley, and Lily all offering to help in any way they could.

After his family was killed, Damian lived in complete isolation for years minimizing human contact. For the past three years, he'd been advancing forward letting people into his life and actually depending on them to do stuff. He liked his small team of smart people helping him invent gadgets that paid in some cases, and with other inventions helping a struggling third-world country with food or power. Now they were all offering to go all in and spend their free time on a case that was completely outside of their job duties, just to help him and his new family of Ariana and Hermione.

"Thanks, everyone. I made some great hiring decisions when I brought you all on board. You are good people willing to help your co-workers and me at any time. I really appreciate it from the bottom of my heart, and I'll take you up on your offers. We need to continue to make progress on our projects, but I wouldn't mind after-hours help with developing a picture of the sheriff's illegal network of thugs. Let me put my thoughts down on paper with what I have so far, and maybe you can choose to work on something that interests you."

His team nodded and he had this silly urge to cheer. Instead, he took the time to make eye contact with each person and express his appreciation. He gave a final group smile and left to borrow some knives from Pete's restaurant to try out Chris's scanner technology. Pete sighed when he heard someone else was after his good friend, Damian.

"How does one computer geek end up in so much trouble?" Pete asked.

"I think this computer geek gets into trouble by using his vast computer skills to help bring criminals down. I'll admit I always seem shocked that they want to try and stop me from discovering whatever criminal activities they are up to. Police departments have a little experience with searching the internet for activity, but they lack the skill to reach the far corners of the dark web, so that's usually the skill I bring."

"Tell me there isn't going to be trouble for my restaurant. It's doing so well, and I would hate to have to close for a few weeks for repairs."

"I can't make any promises, but I think your restaurant is safe. I've done just a little research so far, but I think this corrupt cop is very specific in her targeting—she doesn't seem to be injuring those around her target."

"Good to know, not that I don't also care about you, Damian."

"I know, and as a silent partner in your restaurant, I would hate to see anything happen to it. That's why I'm borrowing knives as we're testing a new defense system for this warehouse."

"So you're going to chase anyone off who has a knife or gun and walks into my restaurant?"

"No. Our software will set off an alarm when it senses serious knives or guns—we don't want the alarm going off for, say a Swiss army knife—and then if we're at work we'll check out the offender. If it is after business hours, we'll let it go. How does that sound?" Damian asked his friend.

"That will work, though I admit I'm curious as to how many customers are dining with weapons on them. Or maybe after this is over, we can use your technology to find the customers walking away with my silverware."

"Is that a large problem?" Damian asked.

"Not really, I'm just trying to look at the bright side of the situation. Maybe you'll create a product that can be sold to restaurants that are having theft problems. Your system for controlling the dispensing of alcohol has been a hit. In restaurant chat rooms, it's held up as the gold standard because it works, and you make it easy to customize it to the type of alcohol and workflow of an establishment. I'll ask my fellow restaurateurs if they have a need for that technology. I mean, if you're having to buy kitchen knives every week, that would eat into your profits."

Damian had discovered Pete's original bar in Oakland several years ago, and Pete had confessed to him one night that he just fired his favorite employee because they were serving alcohol free to their friends. He had no way to sense whether an employee was prone to doing that during the interview process and that had led him to fire some of his best employees. Damian asked for a tour of the bar and where the alcohol was stored as well as storage spaces around the bar. He then went back to his island and worked on a solution for Pete. His first installation was rather crude, but the idea proved itself. An employee had to enter their identification and a customer tab to get any alcohol dispensed. Pete's problem was solved, and he'd been able to contact a few employees that he fired but liked and offer them back their jobs knowing they couldn't succumb to friend pressure and dispense a free drink. Damian spent the next several months making the system prettier so that it fit with either silver or brass décor rather than the original ugly white PVC pipe he started with. Within eight months, he'd been inundated with requests from other bars and restaurants to install the system. He eventually sold his invention to a restaurant supply company. Pete's restaurant remained the free installation and where he worked through any improvements that he would use to update his original product.

"I think that is a problem for some restaurants, but not mine. I'll admit I'm curious to see what kind of weapons my patrons bring to my restaurant."

"I'll bring your knives back in a few hours. It shouldn't take us long to see if this technology works," Damian said as he walked away to return to his office. He gave the knives and a water gun to Chris and Haley as they were working on the project together.

He had a conversation with Ariana later that afternoon. She called his work phone from one of her start-up company's work phones. She had new cellphones for Hermione and herself and passed the numbers on to Damian. She was using the phone call software to check texts and phone calls, so while it was an inconvenience, it wasn't the end of the world.

# CHAPTER 6

amian returned to Red Rock Island. He checked that both his house and Ariana's house had all security systems operational. Ariana didn't always fuss over security, but the scare they had while Hermione was driving was enough of a reminder to turn all her security features on. He went outside to fish for both his dinner and that of his cats. He was relieved not to be intruded upon by a drone. Over the years, he had learned that his time spent fishing was very relaxing and contemplative for him—it was his version of yoga.

A few hours later he wrapped up dinner for himself and the cats and had his usual nighttime conversation with Ariana and Hermione to catch up on their lives. He checked on the progress he and his team were making on documenting Sheriff Wendy Knight's movement of money for the past twenty years. While it was taking more time to get the older information, the sheriff was likely more careless about leaving a trail at the start of her white-collar crime career. It was only recently that she graduated from white-collar crime to felonies. He and his team were gathering pieces of evidence. It was enough to confirm her illegal activity, but Damian had aspirations of detailing a far greater crime wave directed by the sheriff. He wanted to capture as many of the associates she used to carry out her misdeeds as possible.

He was woken by alarms shortly after one o'clock in the morning. He sat up in bed, grabbing his tablet to assess what was going on. He sprang out of his bed and ran down to his lab. Both his house and Ariana's were under attack. He knew she would have alarms sounding in her house, but still, the first call he made was to her.

"We're safe at the moment and the Belvedere police are on their way. Hello to you," Ariana answered the phone call.

"My house is under attack as well. Is Hermione awake and assisting you?"

"Trust me when I say that even a teenager can't sleep through the noise of the security alarm. She's using the laptop to shoot various substances at the intruders, and judging by her laughter, her aim has been good. I turned off the audio alarms as there's no need to wake up all of my neighbors, but I like the bright spotlights you installed. It makes it very easy for us to see these intruders. I hear a siren in the distance, so help is on its way. I think my intruders may have heard it as well as they seem to be packing up."

"That's good news. Text me with updates. I'm going to go to work on these fools who think they can breach my island."

"Since my intruders are running away, do you want Hermione to take over some of the technology at your house?"

"Sure, I'll send her a link. She can operate the water cannons situated around the island. My guys arrived wearing wetsuits and facemasks, apparently thinking that will be enough to avoid being damaged by the cannons. Little do they know that I can turn up the pressure enough that it will pierce their wetsuits. I don't intend to do that as I don't want to cause serious long-term damage to any of these intruders, but I do plan to make them uncomfortable. Talk to you soon. Stay safe and I love you."

Damian took another look at Ariana's house to confirm that

her intruders were on the retreat. He sent Hermione a link to operate the lower water cannons after first turning up the pressure on them. He spent a few more seconds watching to see that she took over and he smiled at some of her direct hits. The kid had the temerity to aim at the tender spots of these intruders. Several of them had doubled over at the pressure directed to those body parts.

He'd lost time checking on Ariana and Hermione. He turned his exterior spotlights on, and his island was lit up like it was a nighttime football game. Apparently, several of his intruders were wearing night-vision goggles and were temporarily blinded by the bright lights, judging by the way they were grabbing their goggles. While their eyes adjusted to the bright light, Damian launched a few drones with some new surprises. Not only did the drones contain water balloons dyed with his famous bright green dye, but he'd added diluted sulfuric acid and the lovely smell of rancid fish parts. Damian doubted they'd ever be able to use the wetsuits again between the dye stains and the smell.

He briefly checked in with the screens displaying Hermione's cannon work. The men were returning to jet skis that were parked on the beach. The men up top were also retreating as two of the four of them apparently got his drone concoction in their eyes and they were temporarily blinded. He knew this because they were pressing on their eyes while being led by their companions back down the rocky slope they came up. As a courtesy, he left the bright lights on so the sighted men had a better ability to get their companions down the hill. Still, it was a slow descent with a few falls. When they reached the beach, the two blinded men put their faces down in the water with the hope of getting the nasty substance off their faces and out of their eyes.

After the last time his island was invaded by unfriendly people, he decided to add a public address speaker and so after he sent the exterior into the nighttime darkness, he turned on his microphone. He was mad.

"Get the hell off my island and don't come back! And tell that corrupt sheriff of yours that she is going down."

Damian's voice boomed across the bay under cover of darkness. Likely anyone at the marina or walking across the Richmond-San Rafael bridge could hear him. He hoped it made the men who tried to bust into his house think twice about making a third attempt. Certainly, the temporarily blinded men wouldn't be back. He felt his phone vibrate and saw a text from Hermione.

*Loved the voice of God shouted out in the darkness. You rock!*

High praise indeed from a teenager. He texted back.

*Thanks. Are the police at your house?*

*Yes. They're talking to A and she's showing them the video from our house.*

*So, you're safe.*

*Duh.*

Yep, he was texting with a teenager. He debated what to do. Just half an hour had passed, but he was too filled with adrenaline to go back to sleep just yet. He also wanted to talk with Ariana after the cops left. He boiled some water for herbal tea and waited for her call. Perhaps another fifteen minutes passed, and his phone was ringing.

"The cops just left. They didn't think they could identify anyone as they wore masks and gloves. Hermione did some great damage to their privates, but likely not enough to send them to a hospital. The department is on alert now for this house and they really admired your spotlights lighting up the property. It was an especially effective weapon as the intruders were all wearing night-vision goggles. We all enjoyed their pain when the bright lights hit them."

"I had the same thing on my island, and while they were blinded, I dropped water balloons filled with a mixture of lime green dye, diluted sulfuric acid, and curated slushy fish parts."

"Oh my gosh," Ariana sputtered while laughing hard at Damian's description.

"Yeah, two of the guys were temporarily blinded by the acid. I was kind enough to leave the bright lights on so the sighted guys could steer the others off the top of my hill. Mostly, I just wanted them to go home, and I didn't want someone to trip on the hillside in the dark and need a medivac to get off my island," Damian said with amusement in his voice.

"Good thinking on your part. So, what are our next steps? Your house is better protected but inconvenient to Hermione's school. My house has less protection, but the police are close by. Should we consolidate households?"

"Normally, I would move over your way, but my employees are helping with investigating the sheriff, so I want to stay close to them. Do you need to drive to Silicon Valley this week?" Damian asked, referring to a region that encompassed San Francisco to San Jose and all the cities in between.

"I can consolidate my travel into two days. Hermione has long days at school, and I think her first track meet is on Thursday at four in the afternoon. She has practice after class every other day. How long do you think it's going to take to collect enough evidence to charge this sheriff?"

"It's going to take a few weeks. She has a pattern of crime that dates back over twenty years. She's wiggled out of it in the past, but I want to collect enough evidence to send her to prison for a very long time as well as her hired goons."

"Can Ariana and I help?" Hermione asked over the speakerphone.

"You probably could, but your schedule is already full with school and track. Thanks for offering, but at the moment I have enough help from Haley, Angus, Lily, and Chris. I think for the time being we're better off staying in our respective homes. I'll add some enhancements to your house, but I think the alarms, the existing weapons, and the police are enough of a deterrent. Do you feel safe there?"

Damian heard a chorus of "We do" from the ladies.

"Then let's talk about this at a more reasonable hour, but I think we're probably better to stay in our own homes." He heard voices of agreement and they ended the call.

Damian took a deep breath and sighed, looking around his computer lab. He was aware that his heart rate had slowed, and he wondered if he should go upstairs to his bedroom to try and sleep or if he should work on some security enhancements for Ariana's home and deliver them at first light. He had four drones at his house, and he wanted to hold onto two to defend his island. Likely the other two were plenty for his ladies as they needed operators. He had been steering drones for a while. Hermione and Ariana had not, but they were both gamers, so they had the skill. Still, he would start with two and acquire additional drones for both of their houses. His latest toxic mixture was a joy to drop on the heads of people up to no good. He remembered what they said about their schedules, and he would have to wait until the evening to train them.

He had a long day ahead of him, and he was going to devote all his company's resources and invite Natalie and whoever else had an interest in joining his staff to compile evidence against this sheriff. It was time to get a few hours of sleep after he dashed off a few emails to inform them of his plans for the coming day.

# CHAPTER 7

*D*amian arrived at the office a little later than planned. He lost time each day going to a different marina, making arrangements to dock his boat for the day, and then getting transportation to the warehouse. He just sent a memo assigning people various aspects of the case.

Lily was his mathematical whiz, and he had her work on the oldest information looking for bribes from the sheriff twenty years ago. Angus was his devious thinker and so Damian had him working on understanding the method of how she commands her goons. Was it money? Or fear?

Damian was pleasantly surprised to see the additional help that arrived at the warehouse. Natalie brought two active detectives with her as well as an assistant district attorney who specialized in financial crimes. He had a few seconds of being elated over the extra help. Then he remembered the sheriff's reach.

Before he did any work, he'd better do a background search of these three new people to make sure they weren't in cahoots with Sheriff Knight. He told the three new people that he was going to research them first before he allowed them to join his team. He sent them down to Pete's restaurant to wait while he let his computer search.

In under an hour, he recalled his new help and inform them that they passed his background check. He could tell they were unhappy with his attitude, so he explained the attack on the car with Hermione at the wheel and the two attacks on his house and Ariana's house the previous night. He also mentioned his experience with Mr. Santiago.

"Okay, I guess I understand why you had to do a background check. Now that we're past that, how can we help?" said one of the detectives.

Damian stood at a dry-erase board and explained his strategy with the case. He had created the flow chart the previous day when working with his company staff. It would be interesting now that he had detectives and an attorney in the room to see if they agreed with his strategy.

"I think we must collect this information for the DA to have a reasonable chance at conviction. Is my understanding correct?"

Damian's diagram contained within it the sources of the information he proposed collecting. He listened as these experts discussed his strategy. They spoke their language of acronyms before deciding that with a few added explanations, his diagram would work for the conviction of the sheriff. Then he added some intensity in case these experts didn't understand Damian's commitment to putting the sheriff behind bars.

"There's an urgency for this to be solved. This sheriff is dangerous, and she's attacked my family. I had a teenage student driver behind the wheel of my SUV when an ex sheriff deputy tailed us from Carmel. He used a gun to shoot at us. We obviously got away, but it's why I've put my company resources to help find the trail of her crimes. Do you understand my urgency?"

The group nodded though he noticed a small smile on Natalie's face. She would probably say something to her team once he left.

"One more question—do you think I should invite the FBI into our investigation? Do Sheriff Knight's alleged crimes fit the definition of RICO, better known as Racketeer Influenced and Corrupt Organizations?"

Damian could tell his suggestion that the FBI be added wasn't well received by his guests. So he added, "I believe that only the federal government can prosecute RICO, thus my suggestion to invite the FBI."

"Damian, I think you should discuss the inclusion of the FBI during your next meeting with the chief and the DA. They need to make the call, not anyone in this room," the assistant district attorney said.

"Okay. Thanks for the good suggestion. I feel like I should pair you with my team members who are the IT whizzes; how does that sound?"

"Let's try that," Natalie said. Damian had his own tiny smile when he noted that the two detectives she had brought with her thought it was a bad idea. He called Chris and Lily into the conference room and brought in extra laptops. After introductions, they got to work. Natalie provided the car license plates belonging to the prior investigators who had gone missing. Looking at hundreds of cameras in the San Jose area and then spreading out to other regions would generate millions of car photos that his mega-computers were designed to analyze. Damian wrote the programs to track the cars from a week prior until two days after each investigator's disappearance. The programs might take overnight to run given the number of road cameras. He checked in with Haley on the drone project and was happy to see that it was ready to protect the warehouse. He also made a calendar entry to circle back to Pete to see if any restaurant owners had an interest in the technology.

They made progress with locating some details by the end of the day, but there was much more to uncover. The detectives were learning from his people about how to search new areas of the internet. They planned to regroup in the morning and start again. The assistant DA was likewise pleased as he could see the evidence of the case they were starting to build.

Damian left to return to his island where he gathered materials and continued across the bay to Ariana's house. When he was speaking with Ariana and Hermione later, the teenager dropped a new problem in his lap.

"Hey Damian, can you help a new friend of mine?" Hermione asked him.

"I would love to slay all of your dragons for you, but tell me what the problem is before I make any promises."

"There's a new girl at school and she's being harassed by someone from her former city on social media. Can you put a stop to it?"

"That's a loaded question. Give me more details and has she asked her parents to help?"

"Her parents have no online accounts and they don't have any phones or computers at home. So when she talked to them about it, they told her to ignore it. She doesn't have a phone. You can imagine how unusual that is and it sets her up for bullying. She is super smart and that is why I crossed paths with her. Her clothes aren't modern and I've become her friend and protector."

"If her family isn't online, how does an old acquaintance know to harass her with social media? Isn't the point of it to get her attention?"

"This old acquaintance knows that even if she isn't online, he can still cause trouble. He's managed to make friends with classmates at our school and so he posts there and everyone knows about the bad things he says about her."

"This all sounds weird, so let me look into it. Maybe I can talk to her parents and explain what is going on. What's your friend's name and the boy's name?"

"Her name is Hope Fisher, and the guy is Eric Baer."

Damian thought this was a strange situation. He had heard of parents denying smartphones to their teenagers, but he honestly hadn't heard of a family that was completely offline unless they had no internet connection. The catchment area for Hermione's high school had a tiny impoverished community, so Damian doubted that was the cause of the no-technology stand.

"I'll research the family and see what my options are. I don't recall meeting a friend called Hope. Has she been over here when I've been here?"

"No, she's never been here. She's super shy and hasn't hung out with anybody after school," Hermione replied.

"How did you learn her story?"

"We have study period together and I've been trying to make friends with her since school started this year. I remember what it was like to join the school mid-semester, so now I try to make it easier if I can for other incoming students."

"Oh Sweetie, that's very compassionate of you, and thank you for doing that," Ariana said.

"Ditto what Ariana said. Okay, I'll look into this and let you know in a few hours what I can see of the situation," Damian said.

Damian was very curious about this family and felt bad for Hermione's classmate. It would be hard to be a teenager in today's world to come from a home with no computers or internet. It would be like you were from another planet.

"Don't forget my first track meet tomorrow at four. I have no idea how I'll perform against the other school."

"I'm not one for participation medals, but in the case of your track meet, I'd give you one. Unlike the other sports you participated in, you feel way out of your element. We'll celebrate after the meet."

They had dinner and Damian trained the women in the use of the drones and left them with supplies of the concoctions he dropped on assailants. He eventually headed back to his island. Once again Damian felt overwhelmed by all that was required of him. Just a week ago, he was happily working on his company's inventions. Now all of that had been tossed aside to work on this corrupt sheriff, and now Hermione tossed a strange family situation at him. Well, he had to investigate her case first.

He began by searching for the Fisher family. Hermione was correct in that they seemed to have no online presence. He couldn't find any property that they owned in the area around the school, so they must be renters. He couldn't even find an address for the family, so he quietly hacked into the school's records to see what address they had on file. He located the parents' first names as well as that of a younger brother. Damian noted that both children were home-schooled before enrolling at the school district. Damian was sure there was a story there; he just didn't know what it was.

An hour later, Damian figured out the story. They were members of an old German religious community in rural Northern California. They suddenly sold a very large farm and relocated to Marin County, which had to be a cultural shock for the family. They appeared to be living off the proceeds of their property sale and Damian wondered what they planned to do next. Sadly, the skills of running a large farm were not in great demand in this region. Something must have happened in the community they once were members of for such a drastic change to occur.

Next, he looked for information about Eric Baer. He was a young man in his late twenties who belonged to the same Northern California community. Damian could see where he was harassing Hope online, and he wondered where he obtained the skills to do that. He looked into Eric's history and saw he had been in two other communities related to that same German religious community. There was no explanation for why he moved on, and as this community isn't filled with mobile jobs, the moves were unusual. In each case, he was offline for a few months, and then he targeted someone, then moved on. Damian wondered what the guy was up to. Was Eric Baer one of those charismatic psychopaths who managed to do a lot of damage to a community before moving on to search for new victims? Because these communities were more isolated, word of his behavior would be slow to travel.

He had to admit that Hermione dropped quite a puzzle in his lap, and he'd do his best to resolve it for her and her new friend. If this secluded religious community wanted him to, he could make life very difficult for Eric Baer.

# CHAPTER 8

After another long day at the office tracking the sheriff's actions, Damian was glad to head across the bay to Hermione's first track meet. He met the coach and she surprised him by asking for more data similar to what he had provided Hermione to help with her track decisions. She wanted to use it for this year and in future years to help her understand her athletes' potential better. Damian got her email address and promised to send the data her way.

Hermione competed in the long jump and the three-hundred-meter hurdles ending up second for her school but fourth overall. Damian found that three hundred number strange as college and Olympic track races were four hundred meters. Someone, somewhere decided that high school students couldn't hurdle an extra hundred yards.

"I'll be curious to see how she views her fourth-place finish. Considering this is just two high schools, she has to be disappointed with her placement given how well she's done with swimming, water polo, and soccer," Damian said.

"I think she'll be okay with this. She went out for the team because she likes to compete, and she saw all the running is helping her keep in shape for her other sports. That's not to say she won't want to improve, because she will, and she'll be gunning for regional finals."

"It's kind of scary watching the four hundred hurdles because if one of their knees or feet strikes the hurdle, they go crashing down on their knees, hands, and sometimes their face."

"Yeah, those kinds of injuries don't happen in swimming. But she knows how to fall thanks to being a soccer goalie, and from what I understand there are all kinds of kicking, punching, and grabbing that goes on underwater between players during a water polo match. For the most part, if she has any injuries from these two sports, she only has herself to blame and she knows that. Besides, so far she hasn't been seriously injured, just a little sore."

They had to wait a while before Hermione could go with them for pizza, which was her usual post-competition desired meal. Out of respect for her teammates and the coach's request, she waited till all of the track events were completed before leaving. In the meanwhile, Ariana and Damian updated each other on what was going on in their business lives before Ariana asked, "Did you learn anything about Hermione's friend, Hope?"

"I did and it's a strange story," Damian said, describing the background of Eric Baer and the conservative order they belonged to. "Have you met the parents?"

"I haven't even met Hope. Now that I think about it, she was supposed to compete today, I think Hermione said," Ariana said and they both looked at the teenagers around the track trying to determine if any of them fit the name Hope.

"I wonder if that's the girl over by the shot put and javelin. I suppose if you're raised on a farm, you're strong, but her track uniform is a little ill-fitting."

"Maybe she asked for an extra-large uniform as it is more modest."

"Perhaps. How's she doing in her events?" Damian asked.

They looked around for the results board and saw someone with the name Fisher in first place.

"I guess she is doing well. I wonder if her parents are here?" Ariana said looking around at the other parents.

"On our left, four bleacher rows up are I bet her parents," Damian said noticing a pair with a younger boy dressed in what he thought of as somewhere between Amish and Mennonite.

"Normally, I'd be tempted to approach them and welcome them and their daughter to this school, but somehow, I don't think they would appreciate it. We need to meet them alone after we arrange it through the daughters."

"We'll talk it over with Hermione over pizza. We could of course ask Hope and her parents to join us, but I don't think that will go well."

"Nope, let's work through the kids first."

They collected Hermione and headed to her favorite post-competition restaurant. Often her classmates were there with their families, which allowed Damian and Ariana to meet some of the other families. This time they were alone, in part probably because this sport ended later than some of the other sports.

"What did you think of your first track meet?" Damian asked Hermione.

"I'm not disappointed with my placement. I deserved it. I have some things to work on, which is good. I felt so unfocused before today."

"What did you learn?" Ariana asked. She thought she saw some technique issues the teenager could improve upon and wondered if they had the same list.

"Well, on the long jump I need to practice my all-out run. Today, I lost confidence in my starting line and so I screwed my pace up as I neared where I'm supposed to leap, afraid that I would step over the line. I thought about practicing on my own by leaping into the pool, but the surface is different so I don't think that will help."

"You could practice your air position into the pool, but I agree that you don't have spikes on to run on the concrete around the pool, so you can't get your pacing right," Damian said.

"How about the hurdles?" Ariana asked.

"Yeah, well there are multiple things I can get right there. I need to be better off the block, trust my pacing, and not be distracted by the staggered start on the track. I know not to look sideways in the pool while racing. I just need to get that same technique down on land."

"So maybe you like track and field?" Damian asked.

"Maybe I do," Hermione said with a grin.

"That's awesome, Kiddo," Damian chuckled, and Ariana smiled as well.

"So what else is on your mind? I can always tell when you two have something else to discuss with me."

Damian smiled ruefully and said, "Maybe you should sign up for the CIA after college since you're so good at reading people. I wanted to talk to you about Hope and her family."

"Oh, did you find something there?"

"Have you ever met her parents?" Ariana asked.

"No. I haven't been invited to her house or met her parents. I think they were there today. What's up?"

"Her family owned a farm in Northern California. They belonged to a religious community that was quite conservative. Just before they moved here, they sold that farm and are renting in your school district. Hope has a younger brother. Eric Baer appears to be a man in his late twenties. I think he made trouble for the whole family. What's more, he has a pattern of doing this at other locations of this type of religious community. My guess is that he's a charismatic sociopath, and given that this type of community is male-dominated, he's able to do a lot of damage before he moves on to the next community. These are small communities and they're isolated, so he does external damage with the internet that they are not connected to nor understand,

and then he eventually moves on to a new community. I can help Hope's family put him out of business. However, they need to understand what happened for their own mental health."

"That's horrible. So this guy is faking it in the small community and because he has more power as a male and he has some charisma, he's getting away with slandering people to the point that the community is turning against them? That sucks! Take him down, Damian!"

"Yes, I can do that, but the family needs to be involved and understand. Would they be willing to come to Ariana's house this weekend for dinner? I think I can explain the situation in terms they will understand considering they have no experience with computers. Then, they can decide what to do next."

"Hope doesn't have a phone, but I'll talk to her tomorrow and see if the family will come over on Saturday. It sounds like their community likely worships on Sundays."

"Whatever makes them comfortable. I can go to their house, but I would only bring a laptop. It would be easier to explain stuff on a large television."

"Okay, I'll let you know after school tomorrow. I'll see if Hope will invite me to visit their house and let me talk to her parents, then I'll contact you. I know they don't use phones so the only way to ask them over is to meet them. I hope they don't tell me God will take care of this situation."

"They may and that's their choice, but if they liked their community and would like to move somewhere and join a different location of the same community, we can help them do that. I expect that the parents are not enjoying their lives at the moment without their community and their farm. They may want to return to it," Ariana said.

"That means Hope will move away and that's too bad. She's super smart and wasted on a farm, and I think she enjoyed the track meet."

"Yes, but likely her family is miserable, and she can use her smarts on the farm to create stuff, but I hear what you're saying. She likely has few choices in this community. Let's meet the family and go from there," Ariana said.

"They may be disinclined to listen to your request as you're not an elder, so don't hesitate to pull Ariana or me into the conversation. We could video chat with your phone, which will probably freak them out, but at least they can see that the invite is coming from an adult. They may also be embarrassed about the rumors Eric Baer planted in their community. We don't care about those rumors; we just want to help them be happy as fellow human beings."

Hermione stood up and walked around the table to the back of their chairs and hugged them from behind.

"You are such awesome people. You could do nothing, but instead, you're trying to help Hope's family," she said.

"Well, it's easy because it's the right thing to do," Ariana replied.

They finished their meal and left the restaurant. Once they returned home, Hermione headed for her bedroom to study while Damian and Ariana sat out on her deck with a glass of wine.

"We're a complicated family and they're a complicated family for entirely different reasons. I hope they let us help them. Living in the Bay Area has to be painful for a family used to a small religious community and a farming way of life," Ariana said.

"I can't imagine what is it like to try and learn the internet and social media coming from a point of complete ignorance. I got to grow up with it. I didn't have a smartphone in high school because they weren't invented yet, nor was Facebook around, but I used email and understood the power of the internet and computing. The speed of life here in the Bay Area must be shocking. I'm sure they've stepped out of the community to travel, but to live here is a whole different world."

They continued chatting for a while, then Damian said his goodbyes, left Ariana with a kiss, and headed toward her dock for the fifteen-minute boat ride back to Red Rock Island. When he got close to his island, he slowed his boat and did a radar survey to make sure that no one was lying in wait for him as he approached his home. The coast was clear, and he had a solid night's sleep.

# CHAPTER 9

amian arrived at work to find Natalie and her detectives at work with his staff researching the sheriff's behavior over the last twenty years. He took a look at the flowchart he had detailed on his dry-erase board and was happy to see checkmarks by some of the boxes indicating they had the data for a particular piece of evidence. That was progress. As he was the king of the dark web, he joined them, half investigating and half teaching the detectives where to look.

His temporary phone rang and made him jump as he wasn't used to the new ringtone. At least it had caller ID and he knew it was Ariana calling. That was unusual at this time of day. He hoped nothing had come up with Hermione.

"Hey, what's up?" Damian asked.

"I think your Sheriff Wendy Knight is at work interfering with my life."

Damian stiffened and asked, "What's wrong? What did she do?"

The other people in the conference room turned to look at Damian given the sharpness of his tone. It was unusual for him.

"She had her people place hazardous material signs on my

biomedical start-up company and it's been closed down. My company's people can't get inside to take care of their work. They do a lot of work with mediums that have to be documented at timed intervals as to the growth of cancer cells or infectious cells. So it's not just the inconvenience of having the business closed, but it will wreck some of the work that the company's doing. Even if she closes us down for just a day, it will destroy some of our work."

"Do you have a lawyer? I would file a civil harassment temporary restraining order against the sheriff to reopen the business," Damian suggested.

"Actually, that's why I'm calling. I have an attorney, but you mentioned one of the judges is in the sheriff's pocket, so I obviously don't want to ask that judge for the TRO. What's the name of the crooked judge so we can stay away from him or her?"

"Just a moment. I should have looked that up before now. I'll call you back in five to ten minutes," Damian said. He would have to hack into the court's IT system and it likely wasn't a good idea to do that in front of two detectives. He returned to his office and began the hacking effort. He had various ways to hack into computer systems. The fastest, but least preferred, method involved sending emails to someone in that computer system and waiting for them to respond so he could use them as a conduit to reach the system. He didn't like this method as someone like himself could trace the hack back to him. However, he planned to erase all evidence of his intrusion when he was done. Nine minutes later he had an answer for Ariana.

He texted her, *Stay away from Judge Claudia Cox. Need any other help?*

She texted back, *Not yet, thanks*

He returned to the conference room and resumed collecting information on the sheriff.

One of the detectives looked up and said, "You know I'm a suspicious guy and I would bet that you just left the room to do something illegal on a computer. Your computer skill is so far beyond mine that you could have done it in this room, and I wouldn't have understood it unless you put it on the big screen and took me through it step-by-step."

"Maybe I just stepped out to use the bathroom," Damian replied.

"I don't think so unless you were scrolling through Facebook and forgot time, and you don't strike me as someone to do that."

Damian smiled and resumed working on the sheriff's case. About the time they broke for lunch, Ariana called with the news that her attorney had obtained a TRO on the hazmat situation for her company.

"Yay, for the good guys!"

"Yes, my attorney said that it was overturned quickly. The judge had someone call the sheriff's department and ask for details on the hazmat situation and no one could provide any explanation. The judge balanced that response from the sheriff against our explanation about the crucial time of experiments related to cancer treatment occurring inside the building and they had no trouble clearing the way for us to reenter the building."

"You've got a good attorney and a good judge. Congratulations on resolving the situation so quickly. Did you lose any work?"

"They're not sure yet. They think if they did, it will only set them back twenty-four hours. So, fingers crossed that no real damage is done. Are you sure that Hermione and I can't help collect evidence against the sheriff? I'm mad that she went after my business in order to get your attention. I feel like sending her a text or making a telephone call and saying that we're not backing down, we'll see her in jail! Can you give me her cell phone number?"

"I'd rather not antagonize her before she's being hauled away in handcuffs. We'll get our moment in court, and no, I don't need help from you and Hermione. You two know you don't have the time to give me. Just know that I've devoted all my employees to tracking down information on the sheriff and I have two detectives in addition to Natalie. Okay?"

"Yeah, okay. This woman makes me so mad."

"I know, and we'll get her."

"Okay, well it's back to work for me. Talk to you later," Ariana said ending the call.

Damian smiled after hung up. He could imagine Ariana showing up at any speaking engagement of the sheriff's to let her know what she thought of her tactics. He returned to the conference room.

"Well, a judge issued a TRO to the Sheriff's Department after they couldn't come up with a reason for the business closure. My friend asked if she could join us as she's fed up with the sheriff's actions and she wants to speed up our effort to get her behind bars."

"That is a rather brazen abuse of power," said one of the detectives. "We're under the direction of City Hall and would get our asses chewed if we tried a stunt like that."

Damian nodded and they all went back to work. His mega-computer had just finished a run reporting on where the missing investigators' cars were seen traveling down the road. He studied it first to see if he'd written the program in such a manner as to have the computer spit out useful information. That was always the first hurdle to clear. He examined the data and was satisfied that he had good data. Now he needed to analyze it to see if it was useful. If a vehicle was shared between one of the missing investigators and a family member, then it might not be useful. He smiled the more he looked at the data. Each vehicle of a missing investigator was taken off the camera grid within a day of their last known appearance. That suggested something to Damian.

# CHAPTER 10

"Detectives, I had my computer search for all road camera sightings of the investigator vehicles for a few days before their disappearance up to a week after that date. Each vehicle disappeared within a day of the last known appearance of an investigator. None of them have reappeared."

"That's not good news unless the investigator got scared and ran for the airport after parking the vehicle in a garage."

"No, it's not good, especially since the last sighting for each of the investigators was on a road approaching a reservoir."

"I'd ask you how you got the information, but I don't care. We'd better get some dive teams out there. Which reservoirs?"

"Calaveras, Lexington, and San Luis. Do you want some additional help from certified divers? Specifically, my friend whose business was just accidentally closed by the sheriff is a certified scuba diver, as is our teenage ward. They are both certified as advanced open water divers."

"You would expose a teenager to a potential dead body underwater?"

"She's in school today, so she can only help tomorrow and Sunday. She can help you search for the car and then your team can search the car for your dead body. So I think she'll avoid any underwater gruesomeness; on second thought, I won't volunteer her. I'm afraid of what she might see underwater and then have nightmares about it later. Good point, Detective."

"I'll call the chief and see if we can work on those reservoirs today. I know he asked me to call him directly as he wanted to do any searches quietly as he feared the sheriff would hear about it and try to retrieve the bodies."

"She might do that. Could you block the road long before it reaches the reservoir so that spectators are prevented from watching?" Damian asked.

"That will work with two of the reservoirs, but Lexington can be seen from Highway 17 and any police activity would be noted. Can you tell me what camera last spotted the vehicle as I believe there is one end of the reservoir out of public view and maybe we'll luck out there."

"You could also put road work signs up and close the road to just the first two, or you could start at San Luis as the sheriff shouldn't routinely be watching that area as it is two counties away from her jurisdiction."

"That's true, but it's so big. Where would we start the search there?" Natalie asked.

"The last road one of the investigator's cars was located on was along Highway 152, and it looks like a car could have been driven into the reservoir straight from a turn-out on the right side. I would look there first."

The detective nodded and texted the chief all of the information including Ariana's volunteering to help.

About an hour later the chief responded that he wanted to send an undercover diver with Ariana after dark to search. As it was dark underwater, it made no difference whether they went day or night, and they wanted the cover of darkness to hide the two scuba divers going into the water.

Damian notified Ariana and they made arrangements for

Hermione to spend the night on Damian's island. Fortunately, she didn't have school the next day. Ariana was looking forward to doing her share of the work to bring down the sheriff and cheered when Damian told her what her role would be that night.

"It's a good thing, I've dived in the Bay many times so I'm used to being in the dark, instead of someone who dives in just pretty blue waters."

"I haven't done much dark diving as I like seeing bright colors underwater. By the way, I'm forwarding you the detective's contact information as he would like to verify your scuba certification before you meet, which makes a lot of sense. Maybe the two of you want to pull off the road before you reach your destination so you can put your wetsuits on and then simply exit the car and enter the water. It's all about being secretive. I'd offer you other advice but I'm sure you're more experienced than I am with this kind of scuba diving. Good luck!"

Damian would join them for dinner that night and then take Hermione across the bay with him. She was certainly old enough to stay by herself in Ariana's house. However, given the immediate past history of the sheriff's goons attacking Ariana's house, it wasn't safe for her to stay there alone. Damian suspected that he and the teenager would play Fortnite until they heard back from Ariana that she was safe and on her way back home.

While they were on the phone, they both received a text from Hermione saying that Hope thought the idea of meeting with Damian would be good for her whole family, but she would have to confirm it after school.

"That's good news. I would really like to help that family," Damian said. "I guess I'll be spending tomorrow at your house if the family agrees."

Later that night Damian and Hermione were gaming—trying a new game called Monster Adventurer. They were slaying all kinds of imaginary monsters trying to gain payment for their battles. As neither had played it before, they initially died quick deaths before starting over. Damian had just thought he figured out the game design and was advancing a level when his phone rang with a call from Ariana.

"Did you find a car?" Damian asked after connecting the incoming call.

"You could ask how creepy was the water in that reservoir at night."

"How creepy was the water at night? Were there ghostly shapes coming at you?"

"Extremely creepy and now we're waiting at the roadside for the Modesto Sheriff to arrive. I found the car, and my detective partner found the body. We were going to take a picture, but it's dark, and the body is bloated. Instead, we can confirm that the make, model, and license plate belong to your missing investigator."

"Are they keeping it quiet or racing at you with lights and sirens?"

"Per my partner, the chief knows the Modesto Sheriff and vouches for him. This sheriff is perturbed that we were doing an investigation in his jurisdiction without notifying him, but the chief says he understands as he doesn't like our sheriff either. So they are keeping it quiet. The Highway Patrol is also on their way as they may have to close lanes to get the car towed out of here. They are out of the Los Baños office, which is supposed to be beyond Sheriff Knight's reach, but we'll see."

"You think it will take a few hours to break free from that scene?" Damian asked, knowing it was already approaching midnight after looking at his clock.

"Yeah, I'm a material witness, so lots of people want to interview me. It's a ninety-minute drive from here back to the San Jose police station where my car is parked and then I have another hour's drive home. I'm guessing I'll get home around five in the morning, but the sleep deprivation is worth it—I'm thrilled that we have another strong link to the sheriff. I may go out with the detective in the morning to the other reservoirs so maybe I should find a hotel down here and get a little rest. If Hope's family agrees to come to my house for lunch, can you and Hermione handle it? You could get deli from the grocery store or something to be cooked on the barbecue. I would think that family would want something homemade."

Damian could hear the road noise of incessant eighteen-wheelers rolling by with their loads. There was a bump in the road somewhere near Ariana's phone that caused the tractor-trailers to be noisy as they rolled over it.

"We did hear back from Hope, and we've arranged to meet their family at noon at your house. Hermione and I will be fine helping the family understand what is happening to them thanks to this jerk, Eric Baer. Keep us up to date with your underwater findings."

"Will do. I must say that while I'm sad at finding a car with a body in it, I feel good about getting closure for the family. I think I better understand why you help Natalie Severino so much—there's great satisfaction when you bring a unique skill set to help the police. The scuba detective was impressed with my helpfulness in murky water at night. My headlamp and flashlight were more powerful than his, and that allowed us to find the car sooner. If he'd been on his own, I think he would have found it eventually, but it might have taken an extra hour or two."

"You've got powerful lights while I have mega-computers. We each bring something unique to assist the police. Despite your exhaustion, I hope you continue to feel personal satisfaction with the day's work."

"I'm going to hang up now as I can see the cavalry is arriving. Love you and sweet dreams to my two favorite people."

Damian and Hermione retreated to their bedrooms to sleep. By nine the next morning they were in their boat on the way to Ariana's house. Damian decided on a simple meal of lasagna, bread, and salad. He assembled the lasagna so that it was ready to pop into the oven and bake while he explained the internet and computers to Hope's family. Hermione took care of the salad, and it was waiting in the refrigerator to be served. He had a variety of teas for the family to drink.

About midmorning Ariana called with the results from her second dive. This one took place at the Calaveras reservoir. This time they made a more gruesome discovery. There was no car; instead, there was a body tied down to concrete blocks. It would take a while to identify the body as there was no ID and the fingerprints were unreliable due to being underwater for several weeks. The good news was that the body was wrapped in plastic and that kept away various creatures from nibbling on it. With that gruesome thought in the back of their heads, Damian and Hermione welcomed Hope and her family into the house.

Damian noted the conservative dress of the family. The father was wearing a suit while the mother had on a long floral dress. Their son was not with them.

"Hi Hope and Mr. and Mrs. Fisher." Hermione pointed at Damian and introduced him. "This is Damian Green. He's my guardian."

The teenager saw the Fishers frown at the introduction of Damian as her guardian, so she added, "My parents left my life about three years ago." It was better than saying that they had died because they hadn't; they were in protective custody and would likely stay there for many years. The Fishers appeared very uncomfortable with the situation, so Damian stepped in.

"Hello, I'm Damian Green, Hermione's guardian along with Ariana. This is her house, but she was called away on an emergency. I've got lasagna in the oven and Hermione made a salad. I thought the lasagna could bake while I show you what happened with your community due to Eric Baer. I also have some suggestions for how you can handle this situation going forward. Let me just put the lasagna in the oven to bake. I hope you'll like it as it is my personal recipe. Would you like some tea?"

While he was talking, he led the Fisher family to the couch in front of the TV. He wanted to use the TV to explain the information he collected. Damian was an introvert, but when required he could go out of his way to try and make people comfortable. He explained who he was and how Hermione had mentioned that Hope was being harassed at school. He had a single slide on the internet, and then another couple of slides on how social media worked. He wanted them to understand that the data was there to see that Eric Baer was a rotten apple and they were his victim. He took it slowly to make sure they understood his points and how the problem they had been exposed to wasn't going away unless they did something. Then he focused on Eric and what he had done to previous communities before moving on. There was dead silence in the room. His timer went off in the kitchen.

"I'll get it," Hermione said, standing up to go to the oven.

Finally, Mr. Fisher spoke. "So, you have shown us that this Eric Baer is a bad man who has caused damage throughout our communities and not just to my family?"

"Yes. Furthermore, he'll likely move on to another community and do so again. In my world, we would call him a sociopath. There's something not right in his head, and from the bottom of his heart, he enjoys manipulating your community. He may enjoy inflicting violence on members of your community. He can do so because you're cut off from the other communities of your religion. You don't regularly communicate with one another and probably only meet for weddings between groups. So he is able to move from group to group without references. Would you say that is the situation?"

The Fishers looked at each other, then nodded. "Our church elders speak to each other on occasion, but when he arrived in our community, we welcomed him as a man of our faith."

"He likely told your community that he was younger than he was. How old did you think he was?"

"He was in his mid-twenties and wanted to rejoin our faith and community after leaving it for a while."

"He is actually forty-two, but he is blessed by a young appearance. I don't know his real name, but I doubt it is Eric Baer."

Mrs. Fisher looked horrified and said, "He tried to make friends with the young unmarried ladies. He was too old for that."

"Yeah, he tried to kiss me, and I actually slugged him mid-body and ran away," Hope said.

"That must have been when the rumors started that my Hope was a loose woman and we were a lazy family that didn't have a strong faith. I was hurt that the community that we had been a part of for over ten years would believe these rumors about us. It got so uncomfortable that we had to leave."

"I'm sorry. Who did you sell your land to and did you get a fair price?"

"I got a fair price, but it made the community smaller as I sold it to a corporate farmer. He'll destroy the land and treat the animals poorly, but we couldn't stay in Bonduel near the California and Oregon border any longer. We didn't like the grief that Eric was causing our family. We prayed for over six months, but things never got better. We were disappointed that our community couldn't see Mr. Baer for what he was, though from what you told me today, it was far worse than we knew."

"So here is another problem that you were probably unaware of. Each time Eric Baer has gone into a community of your faith, he's targeted a family and made them so uncomfortable that they left. Each time that family has sold the land to the same corporate farming company. He's made a tidy profit with each purchase. Everyone in your community wants to hold onto your farmland. You believe that the farm represents the strength of your family, your community, and your religion, so why would you ever sell it? Nothing that Mr. Baer has done is illegal. However, he's forcing families to give up their farms and move away from their religious communities and that's a moral crime, would you not agree?"

Damian asked. He'd given a lot of thought before he met the Fishers about how to meet them on their level.

"Yes, what you say is true. What can we do? We already sold our land, and we cannot afford to buy it back."

"In researching Mr. Baer, I compiled the list of all the communities in the United States and Canada. If you would like to return to your religious community but in a different state or country, I can provide you with information on property availability in those communities. Furthermore, I would like to contact the elder structure of your religion and meet with those elders to explain what a predator Mr. Baer is, what his motives are, and how they need to guard against the loss of farmland within your religious community. Do you think that is possible? How do I approach them? Maybe we can discuss that over lunch?" Damian said, gesturing everyone to the table which had already been set. He'd read about the customs of this community, and he expected a prayer before the meal and the desire to pass food around rather than fill the plates at the kitchen counter and have everyone sit down.

The Fishers sat at the table as he and Hermione placed the food and serving utensils on it. Damian sat at the head of the table and said, "Mr. Fisher, would you like to lead us in prayer?"

He said the prayer that Damian expected to hear and he smiled to himself when he heard that he and Hermione were specifically blessed. That was his indication that the Fishers trusted and respected him. He knew he wasn't supposed to continue a serious conversation while they ate, so instead, he asked about Hope.

"I understand from Hermione that your daughter is quite smart. Have you looked into college for her?" Damian couldn't imagine talking over Hermione's head about what his plans for her future were, but this was a different culture, and the parents did indeed decide and direct their children to education and apprenticeship opportunities.

"Hope did really well in our Bonduel school. She always had

the best grades, so we would have sent her to get her teaching degree or nursing. We always need more nurses in our community. I haven't thought about that since we moved here as life has been so foreign for us. I really hope we can find a new community of our faith," Mrs. Fisher said.

It was the first thing she had said that day, and her statement told Damian that while they had different views on their cultures, she was trusting him to help them out of their situation. Damian turned the conversation to organic farming as he was interested in understanding their growing methods. They finished the meal and offered to clean up, but Damian insisted they go back and look at the information he had collected.

"I live on the other side of the bay, but once you go home and talk about the information I've provided you with and you have more questions, just ask Hope to get in touch with Hermione and we can go over whatever is causing confusion. I've printed a list of all the communities of your religious faith in the United States and Canada. I've added columns with the name of the community leader, the cost of an acre of land in that community, the size of the community, and whether it's growing. Is there anything else you would like to know about?"

"Would you be able to add the type of religious community? We have eighteen different types. We would also like to be somewhat close to the nursing schools for our community. There is one in Illinois and one in Virginia. So concentrate in those two states. We can take a train to reach the town," Mrs. Fisher said, smiling at her daughter. It was the first time she smiled since she arrived.

"I can do that. How would you suggest I approach your community's leaders to stop Eric Baer from doing more damage? I will shut him down on the internet, but I'm worried he'll move to a new community and create circumstances that will force another family to sell their farm."

"I don't know how to reach the church, but my brother-in-law was devastated when he heard we were leaving our community. His father is an elder in his community. Let's start there. My sister and brother live in Oregon near Salem. Would it be possible for you to travel to Salem by train with me, Mr. Green?" asked Mr. Fisher.

"Would you mind flying there? I have a private plane that will get us there quickly. I'm assisting the police with a case, and I can't afford the time it would take on the train at the moment. All of you would be welcome aboard the plane if you would like to catch up with your family—there's room."

Mrs. Fisher's eyes began watering and Mr. Fisher rubbed her back and turned her head into his shoulder. "Dear, we've been praying for an answer to our problems, and I think our prayers have been answered. Mr. Green, we will keep you and Hermione and Hermione's other guardian—Ariana, I believe you said was her name—in our prayers for the rest of our lives."

"Thank you, Mr. and Mrs. Fisher. I just want to do right by you and your culture and put an end to Mr. Baer's predatory behavior toward your community's women and your land. Just knowing that I'm able to put him out of business is all the thanks I need. I just need that connection to your community to make sure that the entire community is on alert. Sunday would be a convenient day to fly, but I believe that is your sabbath. What day should we visit your family? Do you need to mail them a letter to tell them of your impending visit first? I can still work on shutting down Mr. Baer."

Damian was embarrassed over the family's gratitude, but he guessed he should have expected it. This family was salt of the earth and was trying to show their appreciation.

"Yes, I would like to update my sister and brother-in-law. They should receive a letter from me within a week, so could we make the visit on a Monday a week from now?" Mr. Fisher asked.

Damian was fine with that request as he had work to do on the Sheriff Knight case and to make a mess of Eric Baer's online life.

"I'll send a revised list of communities in Illinois and Virginia on Monday. I'll have Hermione bring the copy and give it to Hope. Next Monday, let's meet here at seven am. It will take us about two hours to land in Salem by the time we drive to the airport and fly the distance. So you can tell your family to expect us around 9:30 or 10 in the morning depending on how far they live from the airport."

The Fishers soon left, and Damian took a deep breath and let it out after he closed the door. "That's a family you don't want to let down. I hope they are happy wherever they decide to move. I think if I were them, I would head to Salem, rather than to a community so far away from here where they don't know anyone."

"Think of how strange it had to be for them to move here. They're a curious mix of the old ways and the new ways. They drive a car, but that is the only technology that they let into their lives. I hate to see Hope go, but it makes sense for her to go to one of those universities. Despite what this Eric Baer did to them and their community, they still want to belong to it."

"Yes, I hope they happily reconnect with their new community. Should we see what Ariana is up to?"

# CHAPTER 11

"*D*id you get any sleep last night?" Damian asked Ariana. "Not much, but more importantly I got a shower and some food."

"Where are you?"

"I called you about finding the body at the second reservoir, and now I'm on my way to the final location. We're taking this convoluted route, so we're not spotted by the public, the media, or any of the sheriff's goons. We're going to have to search a wider area at this reservoir."

"Are you doing okay? Are you holding up?" Damian asked.

"I'm so excited about contributing to this case against the sheriff that none of this is bothering me. I'll admit that it helps that I haven't seen any dead bodies underwater. There was the one wrapped in plastic, but I couldn't see the human inside. I think if I came upon them suddenly, I'd be spooked and have nightmares, but so far, the detective has had to deal with the body, not me. These reservoirs might be the strangest bodies of water I've scuba dived in. There are few fish and a fair amount of garbage. I should be done in about two hours and will head for home. How did your meeting with the Fishers go?"

"I'll admit it was awkward at first. I tried to win them over with a home-cooked meal of lasagna, garlic bread, salad, and tea. I explained the situation and I forgot to tell you about who Eric Baer works for—a corporate farm company. While the company is paying fair market value, the Fishers and, I suspect, the families before them wouldn't have sold the land. For his efforts, Eric has a nice bonus sent to his bank account. So not only does he tear apart these communities, he makes a profit doing so. Mr. Fisher is contacting his sister and brother-in-law in Salem so that I can reach the communities through their elders and warn them about the man's behavior. I'll arrange a private plane to take us to Salem a week from this coming Monday. Can you join us?"

"Let me look at my calendar. I don't recall anything that I can't reschedule that day," Ariana said, and then there was a pause, and she looked the day up on her phone. "I'm good. Where are we meeting?"

"Your house at seven. Between driving to the airport and flying north, we won't get there until probably ten, and I don't know how close the community is to the airport. It's not likely to be close."

"Will they accept what you say? Do they understand enough about computers to get a glimmer of what's going on?"

"What has really got them on board was the land sales that I could demonstrate. After this meeting, they're planning to move to Illinois or Virginia to another of this religion's communities. They wish Hope to attend a nursing program taught by a church-sponsored university, and that's where the two schools are located."

"Wow, your day was almost as interesting as mine and you served a meal in the middle of it. I'm so proud of you wanting to help a strange family in a way that probably only you can do. Are there leftovers for me for dinner tonight? After three dives, I'll need a big plate of delicious carbohydrates. We're getting close to our destination, got to run," she said, clicking off the phone.

"I don't know who is having a weirder day, Ariana or us," Hermione said.

"We aren't having a weird day so much as learning about the cultural norms of a religious community that we'll likely never join. It's a good experience and they were very nice people."

"Yes, but I was dying to say to Hope that she could be anything. Nursing is a great profession, but with her brains she should aim for medical school or be an astronaut or something."

"Remember that her religion and community are very important to her, and she'll be fulfilled by being a nurse and serving her community or helping on a mission. I'm not frustrated for Hope as I think she'll be doing what she wants to do. It's great to come across really nice people."

"Yeah, you're right. Can I come to Salem?"

"Do you have a track meet or any tests that day?"

"No."

"Then I'd prefer that you come as I don't like leaving you alone to face the sheriff's minions yourself. Let me know what I have to do to take you out of school that day. I don't know how Hope's parents feel, but let them know that you're coming and Hope and her brother are welcome to join us as long as they don't mind them missing a school day."

"Will do. Thank you, Damian, for helping them."

"Of course. Let me make those modifications they asked for about other communities of their religion in Virginia and Illinois. I think I might throw Oregon in as well in case they change their minds after meeting up with family. Once Hope graduates from college, there's no reason to stay in one of those states except they will have bought land. Seems far better to me for them to stay on the west coast. I'd hate to have to learn new farming methods based on the climates in those two states, but what do I know?"

"I'm with you there. College is temporary. I don't care what state a college is in, it's what you do after you graduate. I'm not even sure what college and what career I want, but I'm glad I don't feel compelled to go to one of just two colleges that are faith based. There's not much choice there, although I understand how important it is to be surrounded by your religion. I'd be a little mad at my religion for how people I knew for many years behaved thanks to Eric Baer. That's really sad."

"There's a long history of people making bad decisions thanks to charismatic numbskulls. You may also have a chance to compete in a sport and that will determine where you go. Why don't you help me with this spreadsheet for the Fishers? I'll take Oregon and Virginia and you do Illinois. Just fill in the columns." Damian added a few more columns based on what the Fishers said were their decision-making points.

Soon they had the columns filled in and then the printer was making noise as the report printed.

"Perhaps the good part of this story is that Hope has learned how to use computers while at this school. That will serve her well when she goes to a university. She'll need to understand the internet to get a nursing license among other things. From what I read briefly about these two colleges, it sounds like they use technology for learning. Let's go outside and play with Miguel for a while; we've been inside for too long," Damian said as he stretched.

The Portuguese water dog was always up for a rousing game of fetch. They were just finishing up and walking back inside when the driveway alarm sounded on both their phones. They locked the doors and brought up the perimeter cameras wondering if the Fishers had returned. Damian sighed when he saw men in black wearing ball caps and face masks. It was a decent disguise as they had just finished being required to wear masks for the pandemic and they didn't look as out of place as they would have three years ago. Damian looked for weapons but couldn't tell if they had any from the cameras.

"Really, you idiots haven't learned that you can't break in here?" Damian said as he and Hermione got ready to defend

Ariana's home. Then Damian remembered he could call the police and get a rapid response here. He made the call indicating a home invasion, gave the address, and then ended the call. He sent a quick text to Ariana not sure if she was underwater or what, but he wanted her to know that he and Hermione were defending her home and she shouldn't worry.

"Okay, you take the water guns and I'll try our new drone feature. Blast away," Damian said, holding out his hand for a fist bump. Then they got to work.

The men were strictly approaching from the road. There were four of them and none of them appeared to have face shields, though they were wearing sunglasses. Damian liked the fact that the water pumps made noise as that hid the whine of the drone. He stored the drones on Ariana's roof and had their bases connected to electricity that kept them ready to fly. He stopped to pick up a water balloon that he stored in a container on her deck and was soon dropping it on the first man. He loved that the man was splattered with green ink, vinegar, and stinky perfume. By the time he hit the third man, he could hear sirens close by and he wondered how the men planned to escape.

This must have been a stupid group of thugs as they were easily caught by the responding police. Three of them bore bright green dye on their clothing and their person. He leaned in to give Hermione a hug and a high five.

"Good job, Kiddo. You kept them distracted while I came in for the finishing touch. Let's wait for the police to come to knock on our door."

He got a text from Ariana,

*Just got back to the car, saw your text and alarm, and I see the police are carting away little green men. Congrats. Should be home in three hours. My scuba partner is enjoying your home defense system. Loves that the men will have to appear before the judge in green dye.*

Damian smiled and shared the text with Hermione who replied, "Tell her it was like watching a bad action movie where the bad guys never had a chance," she said, grinning. He passed on the teenager's message and then got more serious.

*Did you find another car and/or body?*

*Yep. This one was really bad. That car was in the water for a month. I didn't find it scary as I couldn't tell it was a human in the car. I guess the detective has seen this before.*

They texted back and forth a little more until Ariana had to end the conversation as her statement of what she observed had to be taken. They also were notified by the police that their statements needed to be taken. As Damian had already made a copy of the video showing the men arriving in disguise and armed, the conversation was short. The officers were in a jovial mood given the dye-stained burglars in their custody. They were especially gleeful knowing the green dye would be on their skin when they were arraigned on Monday.

Damian knew that he and Hermione needed to chill out before he could do boring computer work and she could work on her school assignments. So, they played a quick round of her favorite board game, which was a great way to reset their minds about defending Ariana's house. After the game was over, they both moved on. Damian went to work on the project of tracking the sheriff's actions over the past twenty years. There was so much research and digging to do to follow her trails.

Ariana arrived home to hugs, and after a quick shower, she sat down to a plate of lasagna and bread while Damian and Hermione listened to her details about her scuba dives and then their stories about the Fishers and the men who tried to enter Ariana's property.

"What a weird day for all of us," Ariana said. "My life was boring before you two came into it. Now I search for dead bodies, while you two stop crime in a secluded religious community."

"We have to write stories occasionally in English class. I might describe today the next time the teacher assigns something. She would assume it was fiction. I mean, seriously, dead bodies in cars and green-dyed house burglars."

"Make sure she knows it is fiction, otherwise the school might bring child protective services down on our heads," Damian said. "Tell her you want to be a mystery writer when you go to college."

"Got it."

"I need to head back across the bay. I suspect that with the new evidence from your dives, we'll be chasing down lots of leads tomorrow. It's amazing how long you have to chase a thread of information on the web. I've read up on how journalists chased information in the Panama Papers, and this is something similar."

Hermione looked at him and said, "Panama Papers? I never heard of that."

"I don't know if the history books will ever cover that story as it is more about financial crimes than history. Basically, in 2017 a group of journalists were given over two terabytes of hacked information from a corrupt legal firm based in Panama that set up all these dummy corporations to hide income from government and business leaders of many countries to avoid taxes. When it came to light, some people were charged with crimes and many foreign leaders were frowned upon by their people. It showed the world how rich people were hiding assets offshore mostly to avoid taxes. However, the world soon forgot about it. For me, it was instructive on how to investigate people."

"That sounds really boring,"

Damian laughed at the teenager's remarks and replied, "Pretty much."

Damian hugged Ariana and Hermione and left to return home.

# CHAPTER 12

On Monday, Damian and his expanded gang of researchers continued working on tracking money and conversations from the sheriff's earliest days. She was brilliant in her criminality. She had set up a corporation over twenty years ago in the Cayman Islands. It was hard to locate as it was set up in secrecy and Damian didn't have the time to try and individually hack into each anonymous account. There were many offshore countries that hosted empty shell corporations like Sheriff Knight's, and if he didn't have a clue where to start, he could spend five years searching for her financial dealings.

Fortunately, she had been careless in the early years of setting up her empire. That had given him the clue to search the Cayman Islands. She named her shell corporation after a street name that she had once lived on. That original corporation was inactive at the moment, but the paper trail gave him the thread he needed. He focused on the Cayman Islands and the law firm that created her original corporation. Next, he illegally hacked into the law firm to see if they handled other shell corporations for the sheriff. Now that he knew he was in the right country and law firm, he proceeded to list all of her shell companies.

Once he did that, he sat back and thought about how he needed to come by the information legally as hacked evidence couldn't be used to convict. At least he didn't think so, and he didn't plan to ask the assistant DA sitting in the room with him if his illegally obtained information could be used to convict the sheriff. Best not to admit a crime to a detective and DA, he thought.

As his screen cursor was blinking at him, he pondered how to come by the information legally. Then he tried to reverse-engineer his findings. He dug into the dark web targeting the particular shell corporations, and the information was there. He decided to stand behind a vague AI explanation betting that the sheriff's defensive team wouldn't know whom to consult to refute Damian's explanation of how he found the data. Besides, he was fairly sure that the U.S. couldn't charge him for a hacking crime committed on the Cayman Islands though they could turn him over to the Cayman officials, he supposed.

"Damian, either you've created the passenger car that will drive us to the moon, or you've discovered the keys to the kingdom for bringing this sheriff to justice," Angus said. "You have that dreamy look on your face that says you're trying to figure out how to explain to others what seems so simple for you to digest."

"I found the original account she set up more than twenty years ago and from there I figured out subsequent accounts that she has had."

"Is it something we can use in court? I can tell by talking to you that you likely can go places that I can't use in a court of law," the assistant DA said.

"That's what the dreamy look as Angus calls it is about, I've got a way to show this stuff in court. However, this is just the first step. I found the accounts; now I have to figure out the money flows—who added money to her coffers, and whom did she pay off? This is like chasing an octopus family in that there are many of them and you have to follow each tentacle. There are thousands of transactions. I'd like to start at higher quantity transactions—say, those above $20,000, and chase them down. If I start with the highest dollar amounts and trace those, that will give you enough to arrest Sheriff Knight, correct?"

"No, the money transactions alone are not criminal. We need to connect the transaction to a crime—murder, bribery, extortion, or something similar," the assistant DA said.

"Okay, then I'll locate the transactions and the rest of you determine how they were put to use. In some cases, if these are campaign contributions, we may have a harder time linking them to a specific action."

"Let's not worry about campaign contributions. I'm more interested in payments for officers and judges and Rene Santiago and anyone else who has been busted for being an associate of the sheriff on a prior investigation."

Everyone nodded, and within twenty minutes they all were running down events that happened with the person who received the payment.

Damian stopped a moment and thought about the three dead investigators. What could he do to give them justice? He searched the accounts and made a list of all the substantial payments around the time of each death. He started following those payments through a web of transactions. Just as he thought his eyes would bleed from looking at financial transactions, he found what he was looking for.

"I think I have it here," Damian said and then explained to the assembled room what his thinking was as he tracked the flow of payments.

"That's really good, Damian. So, she hired the Asian Warriors gang to do her dirty work. She probably has her deputies turning a blind eye to illegal gambling or drugs as they fund the gang with both. Still, we can see she made a payment to the gang. How do I prove it was for the express purpose of killing an investigator?"

"I think that it is up to the DA and the police to get a confession from the gang members who carried out the murders. Let me look into how much the gang has had to pay the sheriff over the years."

That turned out to be an enlightening review. The gang was paying a large amount to the sheriff each year. The revelations were so powerful that the assistant DA asked for a meeting of the committee that afternoon or evening. The meeting time was set for four that afternoon, which meant that given the traffic pattern Damian and Natalie's crew should wrap up and leave soon. Damian would leave his staff behind and travel with Natalie, and she would bring him back to the marina where his boat was docked.

Damian packed his computer and his gym bag of weapons in case they were needed. The two detectives and the assistant DA cars traveled with them. They were all rather lead-footed and quickly moved south.

"Have you noticed if anyone has been tailing you to my office each day?" Damian asked Natalie.

"I've thought a few times that I'm being tailed, but then I'll daydream while I'm driving, look back in my rearview mirror, and discover that they are not there."

"I have surprises if anyone gets in our way, and I'll be watching."

"I can't believe that sheriff would be so bold as to take down a retired detective."

"Remember that all three bodies found by Ariana were police investigators, so we know she has the balls to do that."

"Have you checked your car for trackers?" Damian asked.

"No. I'm not as suspicious as you are."

"Okay, let me see if I can scan your car from the inside for a tracking device," Damian said as he pulled a device from the duffle bag at his feet. He turned it on and quickly discovered a device tucked into her moon-roof cover.

"I'm going to call the other cars and let them know we're getting off the freeway for a momentary stop to dispose of a tracking device. Get off at the next exit, as I would like to scan the entire car and that is not easy to do next to the noise on the shoulder."

Natalie did as he asked and he notified the other two cars of his finding. They also wanted their cars scanned, so they all pulled into a parking area of a strip mall. Damian pulled the device from Natalie's roof and began scanning the remainder of the car. There was just the one tracker. He then scanned the other two cars and found additional trackers. He hadn't paid attention to what off-ramp Natalie had chosen. He did so now and found they were in Alameda County and in theory safe from the sheriff. He debated what to do with the trackers and decided he wanted to find a couple of tractor-trailers to put them on as once the sheriff's tracker caught up to the semi-truck, they would know the trackers were discovered and moved. After looking around for some large trucks, he quickly moved the trackers over to a few trucks parked at a nearby loading dock. They were soon back on the freeway, though the afternoon traffic rush was building and they were only moving about thirty-five miles an hour. With the road so congested with cars, it was hard to tell if they were being followed.

The car entered the boundaries of Santa Clara County and the jurisdiction of Sheriff Knight. Damian had his bag of devices at his feet and the zipper open. They were about five miles from the meeting location when the lights of a law enforcement vehicle started flashing behind them. Damian looked back and saw three cars obviously with the intent of escorting Natalie's car off the freeway.

"What should we do? I could pull over to the side of the road where everybody on the freeway is watching, but they could put us in handcuffs and haul us away and shoot us at a different location."

"Call your chief and maybe your former department can send cars or a helicopter to our location. Meanwhile, I'm going to launch a drone and have it drop something on the sheriff's windshield. I agree that we don't want to exit the freeway and we don't want to come to a stop."

He heard Natalie dial someone in the department to get help. Meanwhile he launched the drone out the window and sent it toward the first sheriff's car. This was a more sophisticated drone than the one he kept on his island as it could carry two items. He quickly took out two of the cars with a black greasy substance filled water balloon dropped on the windshield. The two cars hit each other and backed off. Damian had to bring the drone back to the car to reload it and he did so. He needed to try something different on the third car as it had become more agitated once it saw that it was alone in its pursuit of Natalie in Damian's car. He had an acid with him that ate through metal. His goal was to drop it on top of the engine compartment and hope that the heat from the engine and the hot hood in conjunction with the acid disabled the car quickly.

"Is help on the way?" Damian asked.

"Sort of. The helicopter will take ten minutes to get into the air and it dispatched cruisers toward our location, but with the heavy traffic it's not easy to reach us."

"Okay. I'm going for the nuclear version of stopping the car," Damian said just as their car was bumped by the sheriff cruiser.

"What's the nuclear version?" Natalie asked as Damian escorted the drone back toward the sheriff's car.

"I'm dropping this substance on the hood of the car; it can quickly eat through the metal and take out the engine, carburetor, battery, or whatever else is below where it breaks open."

Even though he knew that the sheriff's deputies likely wanted to kill him and Natalie, he didn't want to return the favor and kill the deputy. He needed to be very precise in dropping the substance on the hood so that it didn't splash on the officer and yet stayed at pace with the speed of the car.

"Slow down so I can be precise in my drop."

Natalie slowed and Damian brought the drone in and aimed for the front of the hood of the car. At the very least he would take out the radiator which would cause the car to overheat pretty quickly. He made his two drops and watched with the camera from the drone. It was taking excruciatingly long seconds for something to happen. Then he smiled as he watched steam bellow up from the car. He briefly felt bad about the traffic behind him. Through no fault of their own, they now had three disabled sheriff's vehicles blocking the road in heavy traffic.

"Score!"

"Sometimes, Damian, you're really scary with your inventions, but I for one am grateful for what you did as I don't think we would've come out of the situation alive."

"Exactly my thinking. Still, I didn't want to drop that solution on a deputy; that would've caused horrific pain and damage. Instead, I took out his radiator and other things under the hood which was a great way of disabling the car. What's the police department going to do with these three deputies, or maybe I should say six as I believe there are two in each car?"

"There will be a police investigation as to why they were tailing us and I'm sure they'll have a couple stories to try and cover their asses, and we'll have a few more names to check for illegal payments since the police report will contain the names of the deputies in those cars."

"Natalie, you're starting to think like a computer geek. You want their names so we can convict them of something bigger than a false arrest."

"It's one of the reasons I've paired with you from the very beginning. I know that I drag you into tight situations with the cases I ask you to consult on. I never have to worry about you pulling out a gun and shooting somebody who's trying to harm us. Instead, you pull out some do-it-yourself self-defense gadget that works better than a gun."

"Better than a gun? That's really high praise coming from a former police officer. I'm going to call the other two cars. I don't know if they saw the activity or if they're stuck in the jam behind all this crap."

Damian reached the other two cars to find that they had wisely exited the freeway the moment they saw the sheriff's cars, so they were still making their way toward headquarters via the city streets. Natalie took the off-ramp for First Street and was happy to see some of her brotherhood ready to escort her vehicle the rest of the way to the meeting location. It was only a four-block drive, but it also went past the sheriff's headquarters. They made it unharmed into the parking structure and through the doors of the police department.

The committee that Damian had previously met by video was awaiting them seated around the conference table. While they were waiting for the assistant DA and detectives to arrive, Natalie offered her chief a report of the incident they had run into. Damian played the video footage from his drone of the activity that had occurred on the freeway.

"I hope I won't be charged for damaging sheriff's cars. That activity helped our case because we now have the names of six deputies who will be looking for private payments from the sheriff to carry out her dirty work. It's very helpful when they volunteer names for us to investigate."

"If Sheriff Knight's department submits charges to my office, I can assure you that they won't go anywhere," said DA Silverstein.

"I'll speak for Natalie in saying that if they had gotten us alone and out of public view and maybe even in public view, we would've ended up dead just like the investigators we fetched out of the three reservoirs. Sheriff Knight is a maniac who needs to be stopped before more innocent people are murdered by her or her henchmen," Damian said.

The other members of their group arrived, and Damian began his presentation of the evidence they had dug up so far. There was silence in the room when he finished explaining the sources and distribution of income in the sheriff's Cayman account. All eyes turned toward the District Attorney awaiting his assessment of the initial round of data.

"If this was all we had, I would be worried about getting a conviction. Thanks to your explanation, Mr. Green, I have a sense of the additional information you're digging up. I'm going to go to a judge and see if we can get an arrest warrant this evening for the sheriff. Given that she is a powerful public servant, the judge is not going to be happy with my request. However, the evidence of the lengths she was willing to go to intimidate you on your journey here today will throw weight in my favor toward getting that warrant."

Damian nodded and said, "I thought that would be your reading of the situation. Do you need anything else today? If not, I think Natalie, the two detectives, and the assistant DA deserve police protection. If I can get an escort to the dock in Oakland, I'll return to work on this investigation."

# CHAPTER 13

Sheriff Wendy Knight paced back and forth in her wheelchair. She rolled her chair one direction, spun it, then rolled it back to where she started. She was not in her official office at the moment, but rather at what she considered her second office—a suite in an airplane hangar at the airport. She'd had the suite for at least twenty years, always knowing that she would likely have to run to stay ahead of the law one day.

She had spies everywhere in the county, both human and electronic. She had listening devices in both the DA's and the police department's conference rooms. All of them. That had allowed her to stay ahead of them every time they got close to her organization. The only question now was whether to take the commercial flight to Puerto Vallarta where she had a beautiful condo on the beach or arrange a more expensive private shuttle. She knew it would be evening before a judge issued an arrest warrant for her, so she purchased a one-way commercial ticket. She debated using a fake identity, but the San Jose police had a station at the airport and would likely recognize her. The wheelchair was something she couldn't hide, so she would fly under her own name to a different Mexican city before heading to Puerto Vallarta. Fifteen minutes later she was quickly through security and at the boarding gate; she would later learn that she had been in Mexican airspace when the warrant came through.

When she first learned about Damian Green joining the investigation, she'd been very wary that he might finally have the skills to dig into her empire. She sent her immediate family to Mexico the day after Rene Santiago was found to be her mole. She also had a company that she ran out of Mexico and the Caymans that funded all of her activity. By moving south to Mexico, she could still control her empire.

Four hours later, her attorney picked her up at the airport and drove her to her condominium. Long ago she had put resources at her disposal including three different vehicles that were wheelchair accessible and that she could choose to drive if she felt like it. Rather than greet her family, she scheduled a late-night meeting with her private organization to strategize her next actions. Those around the table were well paid and just as guilty of criminal activity as she was. Furthermore, she had been at this game long enough to make sure the Mexican authorities were on her side too. When she purchased the beachside condominium, she also purchased an additional unit that she converted entirely into offices. She now wheeled herself into those offices for the meeting.

It had been a long day, and there were always microaggressions in regard to her wheelchair. Sometimes people tried to push her chair from the back as though she was helpless. She hated the times when she had to wait in the plane for someone to bring her wheelchair to her as it didn't fit in the overhead storage. At least she was saved the indignities at security as her reputation got her through without a search.

She entered the room and poured herself a drink and then wheeled herself over to the head of the table.

"I never thought a computer geek would have any defense whatsoever against my people. Not only has he successfully resisted attempts to kill him, but he's injured my loyal deputies along the way. Tell me what happened on the freeway—it should have been so easy to eliminate him. Instead, a warrant has been issued for my arrest."

"Mr. Green apparently figured out your strategy and came prepared to protect himself. When our agent planned to gun him down in Half Moon Bay, he threw water balloons at that car. Those water balloons contained a mixture of grease and something black which quickly blocked the windshield, and it can't be cleaned off with washer fluid, so today two of our cars hit each other when they couldn't see. This afternoon he used the drone to drop those balloons with the greasy black stuff on our cars. He then brought the drone back in and loaded it with something in glass. That something was a powerful acid that simply melted through the hood of the cruiser and destroyed the radiator, so that killed the car on the freeway. We planned to pick up his car on the city streets, but the San Jose Police Department had their own cruisers waiting on the off-ramp to escort him to the meeting."

"Did you follow him home?"

"We tried, but they knew we were likely to follow them, and they had a police cruiser providing escort. We gave up as they were approaching Oakland."

"All of your men have failed at attacks on his home, his car, and his girlfriend's home. How else can we threaten him?"

"We discovered his office location, though he probably has the same technology there. He seems to make the stuff and sell it as a product. How about the girlfriend? And is there a daughter? Could we kidnap her and hold her hostage to make him stop his investigation?"

"I'll have to connect with a gang and pay money for that. Our guys don't like harming kids. Also, we'll have to hold her somewhere and this guy will move heaven and earth for the girl."

"Do our guys understand that this man is not only going to

send me to prison for a long time, but many of you are going also?" Wendy said. "You've either committed a crime or you're an accessory. So, it's to our advantage that we put an end to Damian Green's work. The DA has enough to get an arrest warrant for me, but he knows he doesn't have enough to convict me. He desperately needs Damian Green's help to figure out my finances and who has paid me and who I have paid off over the decades. This is an urgent problem we all need to solve; otherwise we're all going to jail."

Wendy was getting agitated. Her staff didn't seem to grasp the urgency of the problem or the fact they were all going down if Damian Green had his way. As it was, they heard from the conference room at police headquarters that the officers involved in the freeway incident were being added to his list to investigate. They were making it easy for him to track her team. Between the alcohol, the stress of the day, and the agitation she felt sitting in this meeting with her people, her face was flushing red, and she was starting to sweat along the blonde hair line of her head.

This Damian Green with his do-it-yourself self-defense weapons had her associates cowed. They were afraid he could out-technology them with any moves they made.

"Well, what are your suggestions? What should we do next?" Wendy asked.

There was silence around the room as everyone kept thinking about different options.

"Could we hire somebody to infiltrate his computers and destroy them?"

"I would think that would take time that we don't have, and he appears to be a genius where computers are concerned. I'm back to the woman and the child. I think we should go after them."

Sheriff Knight didn't care who was in her way; she wanted them dead for interfering with her empire. She just needed the people in this room to find their courage and do the right thing for the organization.

One of the men who had been with her for the past two decades and who also had a very nice condominium in this tower nodded.

"I don't believe we've gone after a child before, but the whole organization is at risk thanks to this Damian Green, I agree with the sheriff that we go after the teenager. Let's collect some info on her."

Wendy nodded at her man and wheeled herself out of the conference room. It was time to head upstairs to her family. Her men understood that they needed to kidnap the teenager to have leverage with Damian Green. It was the only thing that would change his behavior.

The remainder of the week was quiet for Damian and his team as they worked on building the case against the sheriff. Damian had a bag of weapons with him at all times, knowing that the sheriff was going to strike at some point. He heard from Natalie that when police officers had shown up to arraign her for charges, she had already fled to Mexico. He could help the police find her, but they would have to work through diplomatic channels anyway, so he was staying out of it.

# CHAPTER 14

After a quiet weekend, they all met at Ariana's house early Monday morning. It was the first chance for her to meet the Fisher family. The Fishers had also brought their daughter and son with them, so Hermione had company for the day's excursion to Oregon.

Damian heard the two teenagers talking and his ears perked up. He came over and sat next to Hermione.

"Tell me more about the incident you're talking about with Hope."

Hermione looked at him quizzically and said, "I didn't tell you about it?"

Damian felt like giving her one her dramatic teenage shrugs and eye rolls, but it was serious, and he couldn't joke about it.

"So, a strange man approached you in the parking lot and said you needed to come with him, and he flashed a badge at you."

"Yes, I knew the situation was a fake because he had the wrong county on his badge and besides the school resource officer would have been with him. So, I pulled out my water gun and shot acid and green dye at his face. I was running late for my class, so I just hurried back inside. I guess that is why I forgot to tell you, because I immediately went into AP English, and I was caught up in the class."

"I guess you have had so many crises these past few years, that kidnapping attempts don't hit your radar screen. Yes, you should have called me from school to tell me about the incident. I'm going to send my nasty sheriff a message right now."

Hermione nodded, aware that this was one of the few times she had ever seen Damian so mad that his face was flushed. She vowed to talk to him later and apologize for taking her own safety so lightly. She and Hope returned to their conversation, while Damian moved away to his laptop.

First, he sent a message to the chief and DA, then to the school resource officer, and finally to a person he trusted for security. He wanted bodyguards for Hermione and Ariana until this sheriff was locked up. Geez, it was one thing to attack him, but to go after his teenage ward was beyond the pale even for a criminal like Wendy Knight. He was also intensely proud that Hermione had used her brains and wits to fight off another crook.

Next, he spent some time locating a private email address for Wendy Knight and he thought carefully about what to put in the email. He knew he needed to keep threats out of the email as he wouldn't want it to derail her court case. He wrote the email at least ten times, and in the end decided not to send it. There was no way he could write any message that didn't include anger and threats.

Instead, he arranged to get a copy of the video from the school of Hermione's meeting with the deputy. He would add that deputy's name to his list of people to be investigated. Sending him to jail was the ultimate revenge. He had a quick talk with Ariana to update her on the teenager's experience and the fact that they would now have bodyguards around the clock as he couldn't risk either to the corrupt sheriff's machinations.

By the time he finished having his mini and silent meltdown, their plane was in final approach to Salem. Damian arranged for a van to take their large party to meet Mrs. Fisher's brother. The community was about thirty miles outside of the city, and they headed toward a church as it was the communal meeting place. They were treated to a large lunch, after which the men listened to Damian's presentation on computers, the internet, and the tactics of Eric Baer. After lengthy questions, they began to understand the situation and why they as a community needed to take action.

"Mr. Green, we appreciate the time and effort you have gone to in order to help us understand the menace in our community. Thank you for flying my sister and her family here as well. We haven't seen each other in several years. When you're a farmer, it's very hard to get time away as there are always animals to take care of. As you know, we're a peaceful community and we're conscientious objectors to war. That has allowed someone like Eric Baer to do us damage as we believe everyone in our community only wants the best for us. I'm also concerned about the overall loss of land in our communities. Corporate farms get federal incentives and treat their animals poorly. They aren't organic farmers, so they're polluting the water tables in our neighborhoods. We have difficulty competing against them to sell our produce as their subsidies undercut our prices."

"I think there is also something sinister with Eric Baer as he is likely attacking women in your community who are young enough to be his daughter. Beyond what has happened with real estate, he has enjoyed creating animosity within your community. I have two goals—specifically to stop him, and help you end property sales to people outside of your community. If you don't spread the word about his behavior to other communities, then those other communities are at risk to lose their real estate and have their women harassed. Do you have a way to communicate with other conservative religious communities?"

"We have a world conference, but that is months away. We have some organization in North America, but the churches can choose to belong or not to belong. Each individual community operates independently, though we all follow the same seven articles of our faith. I will write to other communities and explain what is going on and ask that they likewise contact other communities. Do you have any idea where Eric Baer will go next?" one of the community leaders asked Damian.

"That is a good question. I can put together a computer model that will predict where he moves next. He's moving to new communities at the direction of the corporate farm business, but I likely could do a computer run of where corporate farming is expanding in the United States and see if any of those areas are close to your communities. Once I return home, I'll run the data on that and mail you the results. I know you have communities in Canada, but I don't know if corporate farming is such a thing given that Canadian regulations are different. I'm going to concentrate on just the United States."

"Does he use the same name as he moves from community to community?" another leader asked.

"He does use the same name. Given that your communities don't talk to each other, he can be secure that one community isn't going to check with the others at the chaos he leaves behind. I'm also going to create a program that will send an alert to me whenever he notes that he is moving into a new community or opens a new bank account at a small local bank, as I think that will be an indication of his next target."

"You can do that? I thought bank accounts were private," asked another community member.

"They are and I'll be breaking some laws by hacking into these accounts, but I do it for the safety of your community. Look what happened to the Fisher family. They didn't lose money on the land sale, but they were shunned based on false rumors. I wouldn't wish that on any family, would you?"

The men shook their heads and Damian thought they vaguely understood what he was trying to do for them. He nodded and eventually moved everyone toward the van to return to the airport. There were quiet conversations everywhere, and he was interested to see what happened next as they flew home. He'd kept an eye on the Fishers and he wondered if they would choose this Oregon community instead of one near a future university that Hope would attend. It had been interesting observing people in this quiet life. No one seemed unhappy, but then again it was hard to read people's thoughts here. It was his impression that this community was more conservative than the one the Fishers had resided in in Northern California. When a family like the Fishers changed communities, he supposed the hardest thing was finding a group that aligned with their values of conservatism.

The school resource officer sent a video of the incident with Hermione while Damian was meeting with the religious community. He pulled it up on his laptop screen and studied the deputy in the picture. He played with the frames of the video to find the best view of the face and then did a search in his database to discover the name of the man who tried to kidnap Hermione. Soon he had a name and almost a resume of data about the person. Interestingly, he was fired by the police department for lying, but the sheriff picked him up and employed him. Damian studied the picture a while longer and decided it was the same guy who along with someone else approached him in the parking lot in Richmond and had likely flattened his truck's tires.

Just one more bad person in the employ of Sheriff Wendy Knight. He sent an email to his staff working on this case to add this new name to the list of people they were reviewing. Angus responded to the email with the comment that they had come up with new data that day to support the case. Damian smiled and pulled up the document that his crew had been working on to review the new data they had entered. Angus was correct, and the new information would make the DA smile. He replied to Angus that he would be back in the office tomorrow and to remind everyone to scan their vehicles and devices for trackers.

He dropped the Fishers off on the way home from the airport at a bland apartment building. After seeing the lush farmland of the community in Oregon, there wasn't much in this apartment building to feed the soul of the Fisher family. After thanking him profusely for all he did for their family and the community, they said their goodbyes.

As they were heading away, Damian asked Hermione what she thought of the day and of the community.

"Their life moves a little too slowly for me. However, I give them lots of respect for the hard life they live without the aid of technology. Why are you asking me? Are you afraid I'll run off and join one of these communities?"

"I don't think I'm worried because there would be no sports for you to compete in. So, if you could get over doing hard manual farm work, never again playing Fortnite, and likely stunting your college career, it's a kinder, gentler life to live."

"I don't think you have anything to worry about, Damian, Hermione would be lost without her technology. Besides, she liked working at your firm during the summer. Those kinds of jobs don't exist in the community we visited in Oregon," Ariana said.

"It's only a kinder, gentler life if you don't have people like Eric Baer in it."

"Truer words have never been said, Hermione."

# CHAPTER 15

*D*amian got word the next day that the Mexican government was assisting in extraditing the sheriff back to San Jose. The sheriff likely had local law enforcement bamboozled, but not the national police. Police detectives would be escorting her later that evening so she could be booked on charges of conspiracy, extortion, and other criminal behaviors as yet to be specified. He liked that last category of charges as he felt like it summed up her life. If they would just look hard enough into it, she'd likely committed every crime known to mankind or had someone else do the dirty work for her.

Meanwhile, his team was doing a phenomenal job building up evidence of extortion and bribery. They were getting closer to linking her with payments for murder. He thought by the end of the week they would make it through the layers of secrecy she built and find her dirty deeds underneath it all. He and the external crew from San Jose returned to speak to the committee about new evidence they uncovered. They made it to the meeting this time without any complications on the freeway. Still, Damian had his bags of tricks with him including a scanner to check for listening devices, something he didn't think to do on his last visit.

The police chief was dismayed to find listening devices all over his building. Damian did the scan in the conference room, and he asked one of the detectives to run the scanning device in other conference rooms and his office. The detective returned with bad news and a bag full of removed devices.

"Did she ever join you for meetings here?" Damian asked the chief.

"She's been in this building many times. Our two departments work on many things jointly. I guess I need to update some procedure that we have to routinely scan certain locations in this building for listening devices. I suppose if not Sheriff Knight, it could have been other criminal types spying on the department."

"She's been in this building so many times that the batteries on the listening devices have died and she's been able to replace them without removing the old ones. If I were you, Mr. Silverstein, I would also check your offices. It's another way she's been able to avoid being brought to justice all these years—she's always two steps ahead of you."

The chief rubbed his temples and sighed. The DA meanwhile made arrangements to have the same police detective run the device through his major offices and conference rooms while they were meeting over at police headquarters.

Damian heard a groan and then an expletive after the chief looked at something on his phone. "I can't believe it."

Damian raised his eyebrows as he must be one of the few people in the room not on the email chain that had all of them either cursing or groaning.

"Sheriff Wendy Knight was arraigned in front of Judge Claudia Cox and was released without bail as she was a prominent citizen in the community and was trustworthy," the chief said, holding his fingers up in quote marks on the latter half of the statement.

"We probably should have thought of that given that Judge Cox is the judge who approved a search of my phone. I have the beginning of evidence to bring her down. What I have might get her chased from office from shame, if she has any, but it's not quite substantial enough to have her sent to jail. That is, if I understand what the assistant DA has been saying about evidence," Damian said.

"She'll undergo judiciary review for this and likely lose her license to practice and her judgeship for showing such poor decision making," DA Silverstein said. "Once you and your group get me the evidence I need to move forward, I'll charge the judge. Then a judiciary committee will evaluate the evidence and remove her from chambers while additional criminal charges are pursued."

"Do you think the sheriff will leave the country again?" Damian asked.

"Probably. You've seen her bank accounts—what kind of cash does she have to flee? Since we extradited the sheriff from Mexico, I presume that is where she'll run back to."

"Not necessarily. She's better off running to a country that the United States doesn't have an extradition treaty with, like many of the countries of Africa. However, perhaps in her arrogance, she never considered she would be a wanted criminal by the United States and so she has headed to her normal second home in Mexico. One problem for her is mobility. While many of the countries of the world may be easy to hide in, with her wheelchair to consider, she doesn't want to end up in a place where sand would impede her ability to roll," Damian observed. "As to her cash, I haven't found all of it yet, but it is in the millions, and she has the funds to go somewhere and live well. Do you have someone monitoring departures at the airport?"

"We have too many airports to watch. Besides the international airports in San Jose, San Francisco, and Oakland, she could jump on a small private plane and fly to another major airport," the chief said. "Here's the real irony: Her department runs the jails and is responsible for making sure she doesn't violate her bail conditions. I'm sure we'll catch her eventually when she jumps her bail. It just makes me mad that she got treated so lightly."

"Let's go over the latest findings from our research," Damian said. He was anxious to get back to work on the many projects he had waiting both at the office and back at his island home.

He took the group through a series of slides showing the accounts he'd unearthed so far, the people involved with contributions and payments, and how they were linked to various events in Santa Clara County.

"This is really good. I'm going back to the judge to get a new arrest warrant and I'll ask for house arrest with an ankle tracker. I'd love to see her thrown in jail, but knowing judges, they'll consider letting her stay at home while her trial goes forward. There's also enough here to issue further arrest warrants. Maybe that will cause some informants to come forward, but I doubt it. She seems to have surrounded herself with crooked law enforcement officers," Silverstein said.

"The election is coming up in a few months. Do we have enough evidence to issue any kind of public statement? I'm sure the election materials are already printed, so it's too late to remove her name from the ballot, but the public deserves to know the story," Chief Swanson said.

"The arrest warrants are public record. I think we need to provide a tip to the media and wait for it to take off. Then you and I can work on a statement for a press conference that we can plan for twenty-four hours later. Mr. Green, would we be able to use some of your slides?" Silverstein asked.

"Yes, as long as you put the source at the bottom as your two departments. I want no public record of my participation. I've trained your detectives and Assistant DA about the sources of information, and they should be listed on the public record as the researchers and can testify in court. Tell me what you want, and I'll prepare the slides with your names on them."

"I'd ask if you're sure you want no credit for the work you've done on the case, but I know that to be true from your past work on our cold cases," Chief Swanson said. "My thanks to you, your company, and your partner for the work you've done on this case."

The remainder of the room nodded and clapped.

Damian said, "Thank you for your support, but please forget my name and my existence. If you want my occasional help on future cases, all of you will do your best to take credit for the work of this committee and leave me out of the credits. My life has been endangered enough without becoming a target by every thug out there. I have a teenager I'm responsible for, and her life has been at risk over this case. Please leave my name out of any proceedings and think of my teenager any time you're tempted to blurt out my name."

There was quiet in the room after Damian's somber response. When examining financial crimes, some members of the committee had forgotten to what lengths the sheriff had gone to shut down prior investigations and investigators. The chief piped in and gave examples of prior attempts on Damian's and his family's lives. He ended with a reminder that everyone in the room was at risk. The committee broke up and Damian headed for the exit with Natalie. Haley's husband was in the area and agreed to give Damian a ride back north as he was headed in the same direction. Damian hoped he'd impressed on the committee the danger and dismay he felt about getting any credit for solving the case.

Two hours later he was on his island fishing for the cats. It was the one thing he could do to relax. He wondered if his name would get out; hopefully the mention of Hermione's existence would make everyone think twice about betraying him. Well, if anyone did, he'd make their life miserable somewhere. He thought perhaps that he and his crew had at most another week of work and they could return to their inventions instead of doing the county's work for them.

# CHAPTER 16

When Damian walked into his company's conference room after another circuitous route to the office on Monday, he was greeted by Angus and Lily's words: "Boss, we found the perfect evidence that will take your sheriff down for a long time."

Damian smiled and said, "Yay, you! I want to get away from chasing this criminal and get back to our normal lives. So, thank you for that added benefit."

"Yeah, well, we want to see the sheriff and her goons locked up for a very long time," Lily said. "I was a bank robber and I served time for my crimes, but her crimes are worse—and she took an oath to uphold her office. She needs to be behind bars, not running loose committing even more crimes."

"That's exactly why I agreed to help the police department with this case. Show me what you've got."

An hour later, the crew from San Jose arrived. Lily again demonstrated the new evidence to them, and they agreed that it was the piece they needed to connect Sheriff Wendy Knight to murder. They passed the information on to their superiors and spent the remainder of the day making sure they documented everyone who had performed a "job" for the sheriff. In total, they had almost thirty names the DA could link to various crimes. Names and activities were added to an organization chart that graphically displayed the sheriff's command of her goons and the activities they perpetrated.

Meanwhile, the chief or the DA leaked news of the arrest warrant to the press, and Damian was amused to watch the lead-up to the next day's press conference. It was reported no one knew where the sheriff was located. Whether the courts knew her location or not, Damian neither knew nor cared. He was happy to return to his island that evening, and he knew he soon wouldn't have to worry about someone invading it or trying to kidnap Hermione out of her school. He had bodyguards around his ladies until the sheriff and her crew were under arrest and no longer a threat. He figured that arrest warrants were issued, and it was taking the police a while to find all of her "employees."

He updated Ariana on the case's breakthroughs that day, and she was thrilled that soon she and Hermione would lose their bodyguards. They had both felt foolish at times having a stranger shadowing them, and both were tired of having their lives disrupted. He didn't know how he felt about assisting the police department again with an active case. This had been a dangerous opponent and only Damian's preparedness had helped them all escape from harm.

This weekend they had a big event with Hermione. She was heading to the track and field regionals which were being held in a city over on the coast. Damian hoped that everyone was in custody by then so they could drive to the meet without worries.

He returned to the island, keeping track of the news, and there was still no sighting of the sheriff showing up to be arrested nor comment on her location. Finally, he couldn't resist knowing and sent an email to the chief inquiring as to how many people who participated in the sheriff's schemes were under arrest.

He responded back that five of the thirty-one targets were in custody.

Gee whiz, that meant there were many criminals still loose. He would have to continue to dock his boat in random marinas and take taxis to work for a while longer. It also meant that both his house and Ariana's could still be attacked. He had trained the security personnel on her house's defense systems, and Hermione was pretty good at operating them as well.

He reviewed his gadgets to make sure everything was locked and loaded even though his island hadn't been bothered in over two weeks. However, perhaps her people will be acting on anger, now that their crimes have been made public. Regardless, he had other projects to work on. Earlier in the day, one of the many alerts he'd set up for Eric Baer had emailed him. He opened the alert to evaluate what the man was up to.

Ah, he was moving on to a new community. This one was about two hundred miles away from the current community. He searched the address of the nearest community and sent it to Hermione so she could notify the Fishers and they in turn could write a letter to the leaders of that community. It was a slow method of communication, but this was how they wanted it done. He debated hacking into Eric's new bank account and moving his money elsewhere. He decided to move the money into the coffers of the local church and leave Eric with a zero balance. Then he looked into the law enforcement agency of this new community to get a sense of how they operated and whether he could count on them to go after Mr. Baer if presented with the right evidence. The Fishers could enlist their religious community from the inside, and he would apply pressure from the outside.

On a whim, he did a search of the department of motor vehicles database to see if Eric Baer had more than one driver's license. In theory, fingerprints are required to get a license, but if he used a clear epoxy, he could change his fingerprints briefly.

Damian scanned the database with his facial recognition software and found two matches. That was a crime.

Next, under both identities, he searched for a criminal record. Then he backed up and decided to search nearby states to see if he had additional licenses. He struck gold in his search and found more licenses. More alarmingly, he found that Eric Baer, under a different name but with a fingerprint match to one of his California driver's licenses, was a registered sex offender. Damian could have kicked himself for not looking at these details earlier. He would print the results of his search and snail-mail it to the Fishers. He didn't think it was a good idea to have Hermione give that kind of information to Hope to pass it on to her parents. Meanwhile, he was going to put it together with other items and see if he could anonymously have local law enforcement take him down.

He was interrupted by his perimeter alarm going off. He pulled his exterior camera views up on another computer in his lab to study what was out there. It appeared to be an approaching helicopter. That wasn't unusual as copters were traversing the bay all the time. Then he watched as someone pulled a pin and dropped a grenade on his house.

That made Damian mad. How dare they attack his house? This must be more of the sheriff's goons. He gave a few seconds' thought about how to handle the copter. When they tossed the second grenade, he made up his mind. He opened one of the trap doors on his island residence and he shot at the helicopter with a spray of his black gunk solution. He thought it might mess with the copter's rotor mechanisms. He watched as indeed it did that and the pilot set the helicopter down just outside of his house. The pilot was lucky he didn't hit anything on the way down.

He called Chief Swanson to relay his situation. The chief promised a helicopter was on its way to his island. Damian was satisfied with that and wondered how long it would take to have the copter removed. Someone would need a crane to lift from the top of his island on to a boat or barge. He made a note to himself that the next time he needed to disable an enemy aircraft, he'd best do so over the water. He was amused that the men were stuck on his island as it was too far to swim ashore in the dark. If they looked around the island, there were no visible boats, and they would be unable to enter his house. Little did these trespassers know, but his house material was bullet- and grenade-proof. So, likely the only damage they did was scratching the metal exterior and scaring any birds away. He was happy that his cats were inside the house.

The chief texted him with the news that their helicopter had an ETA of fifteen minutes, but that the Marin County sheriff was sending a boat as well. He waited for the approach of the police helicopter and then turned on his bright exterior lights. His island was glowing in the dark. He saw that it was unlikely the police helicopter could land given the position of the other one. Still, they could hover and subdue the two men on his island until the boat arrived. According to the chief, the boat was another ten minutes out. Damian had no plan to go outside until the men were searched and in handcuffs. The chief gave Damian's cell phone number to both the police helicopter team and the sheriff's boat.

He spoke with the pilot about what he could do from the ground including shooting the men with water and dye. He debated offering the sheriff his dock, but that meant that they would walk through his house with the prisoners to get them onto the boat and he had a real aversion to that. So he decided to direct them to the beach and offered to have them use the chairlift up the hillside. They agreed to try it as it would be the easiest way to get their prisoners down. As Damian shared the video feed of the men in the first copter dropping grenades on his house, they were caught red-handed. The only question for the approaching sheriff's unit was whether they were armed. He suspected the police helicopter was taking care of that. Wouldn't the men feel hopeless that there was nowhere to run? They would need to be regular and strong swimmers to dive into the bay and swim the three miles to shore when the water temperature was just over fifty degrees. They would have to worry about hypothermia.

Damian watched and listened as the helicopter advised the men where to put their weapons and where to stand waiting for the arrival of the sheriff's boat. The helicopter was able to lower one of its officers to his island, who held the men at gunpoint. Damian informed them that he would be going outside to assist the boat's occupants up his hill. He also warned them he was carrying a water pistol filled with pepper juice as he was not taking any chances with the men. He repeated the message over the PA to make sure the criminals knew not to mess with him, and the lone police officer knew that his weapon was a water gun and not one with bullets in it.

By the time he crossed over the hillside and walked down the hill where his beach was located, the sheriff's boat was extending a ramp to move from the boat to the sand. After introductions, Damian brought the officers up his hillside in his chairlift and then followed. The helicopter above and the deputies in the boat had seen the video of the men tossing grenades at his house. The sheriff's henchmen were handcuffed and read their rights. The deputies gave the all-clear to the helicopter and it lifted up the officer it had lowered, as they planned to return to their base. A crime scene team would be out in the morning to collect evidence. Damian approached his chairlift with the deputies and the first deputy went down the lift, then the two prisoners, and finally the other two deputies went down.

Ten minutes later peace, the lapping of waves, and fog were Damian's companions. He looked at the helicopter taking up space on his front lawn and wondered how they would get it off his island. It looked like a giant firefly sitting on his lawn. He went back inside and shut the lights off. He dropped a text to Ariana describing his adventures that night and reminding her to stay alert as well as sent a text to the bodyguards. It took a while to relax as he was obsessing about the best way to remove the copter. Eventually, with the aid of a good thriller, he finally fell asleep.

125

# CHAPTER 17

*S*end *me a picture of your helicopter* was the text message waiting for him from Ariana when he woke up. He smiled and went outside to take a picture. There was a giant awkward bird sitting in front of his door. He looked around for the pieces of grenade and saw tuffs of grass missing, but it looked like his house hadn't so much as a scratch. He didn't know if that was due to poor aim or poor timing, or if his house's exterior stood as advertised by the manufacturer. He sent Ariana the video.

When he'd built his house with so much protection around and inside it, he had the escaped prisoner that murdered his family in mind. He had no idea when he designed and sourced materials that one day he would be assisting the police and that would bring criminals to disturb the peace of his home.

*OMG! Was anything damaged?*

*Amazingly no, but I'm going to have a crime scene team here today and then I've been thinking about how to remove the bird. I think they'll have to use a helicopter to lift it.*

*Hermione says "hello" and "cool." The cool refers to your house with-*

*standing the grenades. BTW, we both love you and are grateful you're unharmed. Perhaps you should have bodyguards too.*

*It wouldn't have helped last night. My house and its special properties are all the protection I need.*

*Were the men captured on the list of people with arrest warrants?*

*That's a good question. Give me a few moments to look that up.*

Damian admitted he should have thought of that himself. He debated the fastest way to get the information and decided to call Chief Swanson.

He answered with, "More trouble?"

"No, Sir. I was just curious if the men arrested last night were on our list or were these new goons of the sheriff?"

"They were on our list as "Tweedle-dee" and "Tweetle-dumb." Seriously, there's a warrant out for your arrest as an ex law enforcement officer and you go and attempt a more heinous crime than the one you're already charged with? The sheriff's criminal enterprise is filled with stupid people, and I can say that without question as I'm getting reports of arrests and bookings."

Damian chuckled and said, "Thank you, Sir. I'm glad our group didn't miss any members of her organization. How many are in custody at the moment?"

"All but three, and we have information that those three might be out of this country. I'm glad you're safe and unharmed I believe our crime scene team will be at your island this morning."

"I know you have an upcoming press conference, so thanks for the information."

They ended the call and Damian texted the information to Ariana. *Whew*, was her response.

Damian was in a good mood when he called his office to let them know why he wouldn't be in that day. He loved the response from his employees when they suggested they could build a drone for him that could pick the helicopter up and drop it in the bay for him.

His alarms sounded and when he looked at his camera, he

noted a boat with *Sheriff* painted on it. He hoped this wasn't a new way to attack his island. He tried zooming in on the passengers and was happy to see San Jose Police Department insignias. Okay, the boat might be unwelcome, but the people abroad represented the team he was expecting. He went outside and rode the chairlift down. There was mist on the rocks of the hillside, which made them more treacherous than normal. He quickly had the three police department members and their equipment up the hill, while a deputy stayed aboard the boat.

He brought his laptop outside to show the team the footage of the previous night and handed them a CD with a copy of the crap show. He then pointed to the grenades and sat in a chair while he waited for them to be ready to depart. One of the team members walked over and handed him the name of the company and a contact person for the helicopter. The company was anxious to get their helicopter back.

"When will you be done with collecting evidence from the copter?" Damian asked.

"Tell whomever that they can move it in two hours."

Damian dialed the number and was connected to company owner. Damian explained who he was.

"Can you send me a picture?" the man asked.

Damian did so and then the man asked, "Do you know if it is damaged?"

"Yes, I shot with a combination of a greasy and sticky substance that interfered with the rotor. It can't be flown off this island."

"How am I going to get it out of there? It's a two-million-dollar bird."

"Yeah, and you rented it to the wrong people. They used it to throw grenades at my house, so I'm not sympathetic. Still, I want you to come to retrieve your property. I would suggest you hire a bigger helicopter to lift it off the island to a waiting ship, or back to your base of operations, or on to a flatbed on the Richmond shoreline. I don't think there is a big enough crane that could get close enough to the island to lift it off. If I were a pilot, I wouldn't attempt to fly it off even if you could hose the gunk off the rotor."

"Yeah, I can see that from the pictures. I'll call some companies now. Do they need to coordinate with you to access your island?"

"Yes. When you have people in helicopters dropping grenades on you, you want advance notice when another one arrives. The company will probably want to visit and strap the helicopter so that it's ready to be lifted. Ask them to call me to make arrangements to visit my island. They'll need to arrive by boat as there isn't room for a second helicopter to land."

Damian could tell by the end of the conversation that the man was despondent with the cost of getting his helicopter back, but Damian wasn't sympathetic to his plight. The owner rented it to someone who had intended to blow up his house and kill him. If he thought about it, he had enough technology on his island that he could have crashed it into the bay. At least the owner was getting the bird back, though it would require a lot of maintenance.

Damian checked back in with the crime scene unit and they looked like they were close to departing. He thought he would go back inside and catch the press conference, then take a swim around his island to relax his brain and release his anger, and then he'd work on Eric Baer's case.

Two hours later, he walked up his beach in his wetsuit feeling refreshed from the swim. He took his chairlift to the top and hosed off the wetsuit, leaving it to hang outside. A short time later he was showered and alert, looking forward to taking on the world again. He checked his messages and saw one he didn't recognize. He read the transcript of the voice message they left him and it was a company that would remove the helicopter from his front yard. Damian was thrilled when they asked if they could do it that day. He made arrangements for that to take place. He checked on his staff at the warehouse now that they were all back working on company projects rather than searching for the sheriff's illegal activities. Life was fine without him.

The helicopter company would be there in about half an hour. They had decided to lower men and straps by air rather than arriving by boat. Then the helicopter would park somewhere on the mainland and wait for the straps to be wrapped around the downed helicopter. A boat was on its way to take the men on the ground back to wherever they came from as they wouldn't be able to assist the lift of the helicopter, then somehow climb up to the copter above. Just over an hour later, Damian once again had peace and quiet and no helicopter sitting on his front lawn. In celebration, he let the cats outside for the first time in almost twenty-four hours. They scampered around the rocks while he fished for their dinner.

He went inside to finish his package for an unknown law enforcement agency in Northern California. He hoped they would take his materials seriously. If he didn't see action on Eric Baer, he would call in a favor from Chief Swanson and have him make a call on Damian's behalf. He debated whether to email his materials or snail-mail them. There were advantages with each route. In the end, he decided to email the police chief and mention Chief Swanson as a reference. He documented Eric's behavior over the past five years and mentioned that while he was there to buy land for a corporation, he would likely assault one or more women in the community. The address he used to open his new bank account was close to a religious community's school, something he wasn't allowed to do as a sex offender. He wrapped up his story and hit the send button.

He decided to relax with a Golden State Warriors game. They had taken the NBA championship the last season and were a part of a dynasty of talent. They had drafted some new players and lost others to free agency. They seemed to do one of the best jobs in professional sports, constantly adding new players to their roster while keeping a core of three talented players.

He was surprised when his phone rang fifteen minutes into the game. Surprised because he didn't recognize the number, but his phone said the caller was the Apple Valley Police Department. Well, someone read his email even though it was after routine business hours. He hoped that was a good sign.

"Hello."

"This is Police Chief Janet Lee, may I speak to Damian Green?"

"This is he, and I'm thinking you've received the package I sent you regarding a new citizen in your area."

"Who are you and why were you following Eric Baer?"

"My ward is attending high school with a girl from a religious community similar to the one in your area. She told me that Eric Baer was harassing the girl through social media and asked if I could do anything about it as I'm a major computer geek." Damian continued giving this chief the story about the Fishers and the research he did on Mr. Baer.

There was silence on the other end when he finished talking. Finally, she said, "There is much to charge him with in your report after I verify your findings. How were you able to access all of this information?"

"I'd rather not say, but if you would like to check me out, you can call Chief Swanson at the San Jose Police Department as I've assisted the department with a few cases. Here's his cell phone number," Damian said, reciting the chief's cell number. "After you talk to him, call me back."

About thirty minutes later, Chief Lee called him back.

"Did Chief Swanson give you a good reference for me?" he asked as soon as connected the call.

"He called me the second luckiest police chief after all the help you've provided Chief Swanson's department. I have a small department here, so I'm going to verify the multiple licenses and the sex offender status, and then we'll pick him up tonight."

"That's all I wanted. I've met with some of the church leaders regarding his scam and they are working on educating their communities, but they're spread out and some use snail-mail. I'd hate for a woman in your area to be assaulted or a farmer to sell off his or her land when they don't want to do that."

"Thank you, Mr. Green. You didn't have to reach out to me, but I appreciate your assistance in getting this predator off the streets of my community."

Damian said his goodbyes and ended the call. What a weird day it had been, but it was deeply satisfying. He went to bed early, planning on reading a book. He was pleased with the day, but still, it would do some good to read a Lit-RPG story. It was a sub-genre of Fantasy and instead of playing a game, you read a story about players lost inside a gaming world. He liked Thrillers and Science Fiction, but he couldn't stand it when the authors got the technical parts wrong. Lit-RPG was like lying in bed playing a slow video game.

# CHAPTER 18

$\mathcal{B}$y the weekend, the police had managed to arrest everyone involved in Sheriff Wendy Knight's case. The sheriff again had gone to Mexico and again was extradited back to the United States along with her remaining goons. She apparently was horrified when she realized that Judge Claudia Cox would not be her arraignment judge and she would be spending time in the jail she previously managed. Damian would have paid good money to see her wheeled past the prisoners to her new cell.

Ariana and Hermione were glad to see their bodyguards go. They were nice people, but stressful to have around. On Friday, they again rented the house on the beach in Carmel as the regional track meet was in Monterey. Hermione was competing in the long jump, but she knew she didn't have as long a distance as some of her competitors. Still, it was an honor to compete.

Hermione drove the entire way, adding hours to her student license requirement. She was a good driver and Ariana and Damian could relax with her at the wheel, despite sitting in congested traffic most of the way south. They caught up on the ongoing story with the Fishers, who had decided to stay in their apartment until Hope graduated about eighteen months from now. They planned to use that time to travel and visit other religious communities to see which one fit their needs.

Damian relayed to the ladies his conversation with Chief Lee. He'd followed up two days later and noted that Eric Baer was arrested and was presently sitting in jail, while the various jurisdictions negotiated over who would take his case to court. Damian was pleased he was no longer free to assault women.

"So what's the latest with the sheriff?" Ariana asked.

"She's sitting in the jail she used to manage. Rumor had it she was enraged that the crooked judge wasn't handing her arraignment; she was sure she was being released again. While I don't like to see prisoners abused, the county has had to place her in solitary confinement for her own protection. From what I've read about jails, it's horrible to be in solitary, but it's hard to place her in the general population as the other prisoners will try and beat her up. She'd make an easier target in her wheelchair. At least she is in the women's area, which is a tad less violent than the men's side," Damian said with satisfaction.

"So, Chief Swanson called me and said we need to present ourselves for a private ceremony next week so that we can receive their thanks. I told him that we were quiet people happy that criminals were off the street. He said he expected us Tuesday at nine. He said he has something with our names on it, so we have to go. I'll admit he guilted me into saying yes for both of us. Besides, I routinely speed and I'd like a little forgiveness from cops everywhere," Ariana said.

Damian chuckled and said, "Admit it, that's your real motive. You think Chief Swanson is going to give you a laminated card that says, "You can't give me a speeding ticket.""

"Seriously, that would be cool," Hermione said. "Maybe I can work on your next cop case and get that pass."

"Hermione, you realize that it doesn't exist, right? As a student driver, you shouldn't be thinking about speeding."

"Give me a break; both of you speed. I'm going to blame you two for the bad example you set when I get pulled over."

"Don't tell the DMV that when you take your test, or they will flunk you," Damian said.

"Please!" accompanied a perfected teenage eye roll.

They arrived at their rental house and took Miguel for a quick walk before heading downtown to eat.

A quiet night led to an early morning trip to the high school in Monterey that was hosting the regional track and field finals. Hermione arrived in her school uniform and was assigned a competitor number. She would have to wait about four hours for her three tries at the long jump. It was fascinating watching all of the events, and fortunately, they didn't have hot sun beating down on them. There were five other students from Hermione's school at the event and so they cheered them on. Finally, it was her turn. After three tries, she improved her personal best distance by an inch, but it wasn't enough to medal.

"Sorry you didn't get a medal, Kiddo," Damian said.

"It's okay. This is a very black and white sport. You don't have referees making bad calls or calls that benefit your team. I simply didn't jump as far as the other girls, so no medal."

"Sweetie, considering where you came from at the start of the season, just making it to regionals was your medal," Ariana said as they folded the teenager into a group hug.

"Without you two playing substitute parents for me, I never would have gotten the chance to compete, so thank you for taking me on."

After another hug, they left to change clothes and enjoy the coastline. It was an otherwise quiet weekend after a hectic month. Hermione drove them home again, not bothered by corrupt deputies.

Hermione went to her bedroom to work on homework and probably chat with her classmates.

Wrapped together in blankets and holding wine glasses, Ariana and Damian sat on her deck watching the fog roll in.

"I am so grateful that I ran out of air in my tank and washed up on your island three years ago. You've made my life interesting, and raising Hermione is a joy," Ariana said.

"I've also brought criminals to your doorstep and risked your lives at times."

"Yes, but you also rescued me and my company from bad people and you gave us fabulous self-defense toys. You have also done a wonderful job with Hermione. You've made her world safe, and because of that, she can achieve anything she wants to pursue. Thank you for being such a great human being at your core. I guess that's why I love you."

He likewise layered compliments on her and leaned in for a few kisses.

They had an early day coming up the next morning. Ariana would drop Hermione off at school and then head south through heavy traffic for the meeting with the chief. Fortunately, she had business meetings with her start-up companies afterward. Damian was taking his two-seater speed boat to a marina nearest to San Jose, where Natalie would pick him up. After his business with the chief, he was heading to the marina in Richmond and driving his truck to work.

After one final kiss, Damian stood up, planning to head to her dock and his boat.

"I can't think of anyone I would rather suffer through a ceremony with than you, my love," Damian said, turning to walk.

"Remember, I'm only there for the laminated card that says I can't be given speeding tickets."

Damian laughed, blew her a kiss, and hustled to his boat and the adventure that was his life.

The End

# ABOUT THE AUTHOR

I reside in Northern California with my rescue dog and cat. I love to travel, play sports, read, and drink wine and beer. I enjoy the diversity of the world and I'm always watching people and events for story ideas. All of my stories are generated by my imagination, I don't use AI to write books.

If you would like to sign up for my bi-weekly blog and announcement of new books, please follow this link: https://www.AlecPecheBooks.com

While you're waiting for the next story, if you would be so kind as to leave a review for this book, that would be great. I appreciate all the feedback and support. Reviews buoy my spirits and stoke the fires of creativity.

Readers that sign up for my blog receive a free prequel novelette for the Jill Quint Series.

# ALSO BY ALEC PECHE

**Jill Quint, MD Forensic Pathologist Series**

Time's Up (prequel short story)

Vials

Chocolate Diamonds

A Breck Death

Death On A Green

A Taxing Death

Murder At The Podium

Castle Killing

Crescent City Murder

Sicilian Murder

Opus Murder

Forensic Murder

Return to the Scene of the Crime (short story)

Embers of Murder

Ashes to Murder

Mint Death

**Damian Green Series**

Red Rock Island

Willow Glen Heist

The Girl From Diana Park

Evergreen Valley Murder

Long Delayed Justice

**Michelle Watson Series**

Now You Don't See Me

Where Did She Go?

How Did She Get There?

**<u>Dog Humor</u>**

Eat, Play, Poop: Letters to my parents from camp

**<u>New Urban Fantasy Series - Stephanie Jones</u>**

The Awakening at Lake Tahoe (short story)

Witch's Medicine (2024)

9 781955 436137